The Lethal Gorilla

Paul Zindel
AR B.L.: 5.7
Points: 5.0

MG

# P.C. HAWKE
## mysteries

# THE LETHAL GORILLA

- - - - - - - - -

## PAUL ZINDEL

Hyperion
New York

For Lisa Holton and her remembrance of the sweet
delight of Mystery.

To my new young friends Danny Ippolito, Joseph
Ianelli, Joseph Sozio, and Anthony Romano—with
much appreciation for their cheerful words and
encouragement.

Copyright © 2001 by Paul Zindel

Volo and the Volo colophon are trademarks of Disney Enterprises, Inc.
All rights reserved. No part of this book may be reproduced or transmitted in any
form or by any means, electronic or mechanical, including photocopying, recording, or by any information storage and retrieval system, without written permis-
sion from the publisher. For information address Volo Books,
114 Fifth Avenue, New York, New York 10011-5690.

Printed in the United States of America
First Edition
1 3 5 7 9 10 8 6 4 2

The text for this book is set in Janson Text 11.5/15.
Photo of thunderstorm: Don Farrall

Library of Congress Catalog Card Number on file.
ISBN 0-7868-1587-6
Visit www.volobooks.com

# Contents

# THE LETHAL GORILLA • Case #4

## Case #4 began something like this:

On Saturday, October 17, at exactly 9:08 in the morning, Mackenzie's mom, Mrs. Kim Riggs (the New York City coroner), was informed that someone had just died from a jaguar attack at the Bronx Wildlife Conservation Park (a.k.a. the Bronx Zoo). Mackenzie, my best friend and partner private eye, called me and asked if I wanted to take a ride up with them to the scene of the mauling, and I said okay. One of my favorite expressions about N.Y.C. is that it's a jungle out there, but this I had to see.

Mrs. Riggs didn't tell us until we were in her coroner's van and heading up the West Side Highway that the victim of the attack was Ivan Allen, one of the most famous zoologists at the zoo—and in the world for that matter. He was always doing guest shots on late-night TV, blowing hot air up the skirts of David Letterman or Jay Leno. You know, one of those people who brings on an eight-foot python, a cuddly baby cheetah, or a chimpanzee with A.D.D. so that Dave or Jay can feed it a banana or a bottle of milk. But unlike most zoologists, he didn't seem to get along too well with the animals—he was always too busy sucking up to the hosts.

Anyway, the point is that there was no way Mackenzie or I could have guessed that before noon on this beautiful Indian-summer day, we would find ourselves caught up in one of the most bizarre, puzzling, and deadly cases of our sleuthing careers. Or that soon Mac and I would end up on the run from the schemes of the most ferocious animals of all—people. It's a jungle out there, all right.

Recording the terrifying truth and nothing but the truth about this freakazoid case, I am,

*C. C. Hawke*

(a.k.a. Peter Christopher Hawke)

## See No Evil

**By 9 A.M. I was waiting in front** of my apartment house when the coroner's van pulled up, which always drives my Dominican doorman, Miguel, crazy because he says the van is filled with the ticked-off ghosts from fresh dead people. Miguel and I always have a few laughs about things like voodoo, clairvoyance, and sacrificial burnt offerings. He opened the passenger-side door and I jumped in next to Mackenzie. Her mom was driving, and the van smelled nice because Mrs. Riggs always sprays it with Crisp Linen–scented Lysol disinfectant after there's been a ripe corpse in it. The last one was a floater they had pulled out of the Hudson River the night before.

"Hi," I said.

"Yeah," Mackenzie said. Her mom adjusted the beat-up gray fedora she always wears and peeled rubber out of the driveway heading west on 63rd Street. Just the way Mac had her mane of blond hair pulled back tight with a black plastic band and the alien sunglasses she was wearing told me she still had a lot of attitude left over from the fight we had had yesterday over our project for Ms. Kaylee Kenny's chem class.

"Hey, Mac," I said, "what went wrong with the project wasn't my fault."

"Yes, it was," she snapped.

"Don't start up again," Mrs. Riggs said, tuning the car radio as we pulled onto the West Side Highway at 79th Street. On our right was a row of heavy-duty pile drivers sinking a foundation for yet another Trump building. Between the *BAM BAM BAM* and some guy on the radio from the CBS helicopter yakking away, giving traffic reports, I realized I had a bit of a headache.

Mackenzie's my best friend, but that doesn't mean we don't mix things up once in a while. Usually it's about who wears the pants. Not literally, because Mac nearly always wears skirts on the short side, and today she was wearing a silver one she'd found at a SoHo consignment shop. It's about who wears the pants in our relationship.

The argument we had had at Westside School was about dividing up the labors on our project for Ms. Kenny. We had decided we were going to demonstrate spectroscopy by passing a current through a dill pickle. We knew from other kids who'd taken her course that Ms. Kenny loves that experiment and thinks any kid who does it is cool. It's one of the most dramatic ways to show that the sodium atoms in the pickle give off a yellow glow when excited by electricity.

Mackenzie had insisted on handling all the construction for the experiment; hammering two nails into a board, cutting the wires and plug off a lamp, and winding the ends of the wires around the nails. "*You* shop for the pickle," she told me. "I'm tired of being the domestic goddess."

"Okay," I had said. "No big deal. I do my own laundry. I can cook. I'm not an incompetent male," I reminded her.

I went to Zabar's and bought a fat kosher dill. I did add one engineering touch: I used a skinning knife and a metal tube to make a slight hollowing in the middle of the pickle. I thought it would let the electricity pass through more visually. I had no idea it would make the pickle do the terrible thing that it finally did.

"Oh, look," Nicole Filipowitz, a junior with a face like a crazed shih tzu, had yelled out in class as we started the demonstration, "now they're electrocuting a pickle!"

Nicole's just one of the Westside kids who are jealous of Mackenzie's and my reputation as practically professional crime investigators. "I'll bet you're going to catch all your killers now and execute them in your own homemade electric chair," Nicole added. "It'll be like one-stop shopping!"

Mac looked as if she wanted to slug Nicole as she stuck the plug into the socket. Instantly, the current rushed through the pickle. There was a really remarkable yellow glow for a few seconds. Of course, the pickle began to burn a little and smell like a cross between some kind of mutant gorgonzola cheese and roasting rodent roadkill.

Half the class began to gag. Nicole screamed with delight and jumped up and down, holding her nose. The smell made all of the class rise and back away, so that when the pickle exploded it was only me, Mac, and Ms. Kenny who got pelted with hot pickle shrapnel.

"And you don't think that was embarrassing!" Mac snarled at me in the coroner's van as Mrs. Riggs swung a right onto the Cross Bronx Expressway. "Ms. Kenny's face was dripping with pickle pieces! They were in our hair. Our nostrils. No wonder Ms. Kenny gave us a C! I can still hear Nicole laughing. Oh, I'd really like to electrocute *her*!"

The van's phone rang as we got closer to the zoo. Mrs. Riggs punched off the radio and put the call on speakerphone. It was the zoo director, Perry Sagan, a good friend of Mrs. Riggs. Perry had been a player in her weekly poker game for a couple of years now, a good example of how Mrs. Riggs does most of her political networking in N.Y.C.: card games and schmoozing.

"Anything more about how Ivan was attacked?" Mrs. Riggs asked Perry.

We were on the Cross Bronx Expressway now, so there was a lot of static from the bridge overpasses.

"As you probably know," Perry said, "Ivan was a

primate specialist, so he was in charge of the entire staff in the new Congo Gorilla Forest here."

"I remember reading about it in the *Times*," Mrs. Riggs said. "It's pretty big. Even you were excited, right?"

"Oh, yes. It's almost a dozen acres of authentic African landscape. Everyone comes to see the gorillas, but we've also got okapis, monkeys, and wild hogs there. The Congo Gorilla Forest was Ivan's dream child. He raised the money for it. Did the promotion. He was even more excited about a new panda project he had on the drawing board."

"So, exactly what happened?"

"A vast segment of the territory has also been used for jaguars while we're building them a new facility. Ivan was a diabetic. He must have eaten or drunk the wrong thing, and was in the wrong place at the wrong time."

Mrs. Riggs turned up the volume on the speakerphone. The static was even worse. "You think Ivan had a diabetic spell while he was in the big cat area?"

"Something like that," Perry agreed. "If he ever ate sugar—you know, a piece of birthday cake or something—he'd fall into a deep sleep. He was narcoleptic. He'd be out for about a half hour, and then wake up fresh as ever. He was probably looking over the outdoor section of the jaguar tract. The gates to their indoor cages are computerized. They open every day at dawn. From what I can figure, one of the first jaguars out sank his teeth into Ivan and dragged him around like a cat with a mouse. John Henning, a groundskeeper, finally spotted him. Ivan was unconscious, had lost a lot of blood by the time we got him to our hospital. We started blood transfusions for him, but he was gone before we knew it."

Mrs. Riggs spotted the Fordham Gate entrance to the zoo. "We're pulling in now," she told Perry. "I'll catch you in a few minutes."

Mac flicked her sunglasses up so they sat on top of her head. She gave me a punch on the shoulder, which told me she'd gotten past the pickle thing. That's the way it works with us. We may be ticked off at each other for a while about something, but our friendship always wins out.

Mrs. Riggs zipped the van around the Astor Court Circle and parked. Mac and I have been to the Bronx Zoo dozens of times, a lot of them with teachers from Westside School. They all love class trips more than pepperoni pizzas, because they get to dump us at places like the New York Aquarium or the Benjamin Franklin Institute in Philadelphia and then just let us run off like lunatics while they have scones and cappuccinos all day.

"Something's weird," I muttered, as we climbed down out of the coroner's van.

"What?" Mrs. Riggs said.

"That they found Ivan Allen alive. Jaguars bite their

prey's throat. They crush the voice box, then keep their teeth sunk deep until the prey suffocates. They don't let go until it's dead."

"That's in the wild," Mackenzie said.

"She's right," Mrs. Riggs said. "You can't tell what a zoo animal will do. Their instincts get muted in captivity. The jaguars were probably too well fed to need a full-course human breakfast."

A herd of bison with monstrous bearded heads were grazing in a north field. We headed past an ornate fountain. The base was a ring of life-size statues of children riding sea horses. Two immense figures of Venus and Neptune rose from a cluster of seashells, all topped by a gilded swan with a spray of water shooting twenty feet high up into the air.

We went up a sweeping flight of brick steps to a sprawling courtyard surrounded by the zoo's main administration buildings. These were all historical landmarks. The oldest, elaborate facades appeared to rise starkly from beds of rhododendrons and ferns. Towering above and behind slabs of copper and tile roofing were colossal pines and other giant evergreens. Half the leaves had fallen from the oaks and maples.

Smack in the center of the courtyard sat a vast sea lion rookery. A dozen sea lions were splashing and chasing each other, leaping out of the chilly water onto the rocks and slides. One of the largest sea lions was barking. I couldn't help but notice a sign that said: ALL SEA

LIONS SPEND TIME PLAYING GAMES TO DEVELOP AND IMPROVE THEIR SURVIVAL SKILLS.

I couldn't help thinking that maybe Ivan Allen hadn't played enough games as a kid. Perhaps if he had, he'd still be alive.

## A Dram of Murder

**Perry Sagan came hurrying out** of the administration building to greet us. He and Mrs. Riggs hugged and made small talk about the heavy A.M. traffic and about how lucky it was that the sun was shining. Then their smiles faded and they got right down to some of the more practical considerations concerning Ivan's death.

"Ivan's death is a major loss for us," Perry said. "I don't know how we can ever replace him."

"Mac and P.C. came along for the ride," Mrs. Riggs said, indicating us, as if he hadn't noticed.

"Oh, yes," Perry said. "Hi, kids."

"Hi," Mac and I said together. We've had so much rehearsal with being introduced and reintroduced to movers and shakers around town that we croon like a professional Greek chorus, right on cue.

Perry looked and sounded a little surprised to see us, though he knew us well enough from the Riggses' card games. He seemed like a pretty nice guy. The only thing Mackenzie didn't like about him was that he used to pick out and eat all the pistachios from the bowls of mixed nuts Mrs. Riggs would put out. He also used to hit my domain, sour cream–flavored Pringles, pretty heavy, too. Other than that he was a very distinguished man in his fifties, deep-voiced, tall, with flawlessly groomed gray hair like that suit in the TV ads who thinks everyone should call an 800 number and take his talent test to see if they can have a career as a commercial artist. Perry also has manicured and glistening clear-enameled fingernails, which always looks weird to me on a man.

We followed Perry back inside to the main lobby and through a green-tiled passageway to the zoo's hospital wing. "Ivan's new panda project would have been quite a coup for the zoo, I imagine," Mrs. Riggs said as we walked. "China keeps tight reins on their Giant Pandas."

"Right," Perry said. "He did nothing but eat, sleep, and dream of buying the pandas. Maybe that's why the accident happened. Ivan was very distracted by one wild dream of his or another. He had handled all the diplomacy and been courting the Chinese government for years. He'd gotten them to agree to sell us a breeding pair. A first in the world! He'd been spending a great deal of time fund-raising and scouting the zoo grounds for a site. He wanted it to be near the Congo complex. He was probably scouting out the jaguar habitat early that morning."

Perry stopped in the hallway outside one of the hospital rooms. "Ivan's in here, Kim," he told Mrs. Riggs. "Maybe Mac and P.C. should wait outside?"

"Oh, it's okay," Mrs. Riggs said. "The kids meet me down at the morgue for lunch a lot. They've seen more corpses than you can shake a stick at."

Mrs. Riggs marched into the room, flicked on a light switch, and went over to the sheet-covered body on the bed. She pulled the sheet back like the cover on an old love seat.

Perry moved to her side. Mac and I stood respectfully at the bottom of the bed. Ivan's body lay there, naked to the waist. He looked as white and rounded as a blob of bread dough. His plump arms and jowls made it appear that he was sleeping poolside at some kind of spa. Mrs. Riggs's fingers and eyes crawled over the puncture wounds that dotted Ivan's throat like a dark scarlet necklace.

I heard Perry suck in air. "Once a doctor and the paramedics had pronounced Ivan dead I made certain no one touched him until you got here," he told Mrs. Riggs. "I made the nurse and doctor—and our high-school intern—wait in the lab."

"The Bronx medical examiner and lab boys will be coming," Mrs. Riggs said. "I called them before I left. I don't want to step on anybody's toes. We usually work pretty well together. After they get a look, I'll take the body down to our Manhattan labs and go over it with a fine-toothed comb." She let go of Ivan's arm abruptly and kneaded the stiffened skin below his jaw. I figured she was checking his glands for swelling. "Where'd you get the blood for the transfusions? What blood type was he?"

Mac and I both knew where she was going with that question; a transfusion of the wrong type of blood would kill anyone.

"Type A," Perry said. "It was from his own stored-blood supply, so we knew it was safe. We require all employees in high-risk areas to donate blood on a regular basis. We've always got at least a small amount of their own blood ready to give them in an emergency. There are a couple of good animal bites around here every year. Usually they're from a larger snake or a monkey. We had a 'gator rip off a hand several years ago, but that's the extent of our accidents."

"I want to do a preliminary check of the blood work in your lab," Mrs. Riggs said. She pulled the sheet back up over Ivan and turned to us. "What're you kids going to do?"

I knew we'd be fifth wheels, so I answered for both of us. "We're going to take a walk down to the Congo Gorilla Forest."

"Okay," Mrs. Riggs said. As she followed Perry out, she had that look in her eye she gets when she knows Mac and I are going to go off snooping.

Mac and I lingered a few moments alone in the room with the corpse. There's always something about a covered dead body that makes me think it's going to sit bolt upright at any moment and say, "Only kidding, everybody!" or "Hello, I'm a vampire." Besides, it was hard to believe Ivan Allen was dead. It's like really trying to get it through your head that famous people such as Nixon, Princess Di, and River Phoenix are really gone. You'd think celebrities, with all their loot, would never shuffle off this mortal coil.

I used to be really creeped out by Ivan Allen anytime I saw him on TV with one of his baby gorillas or infant baboons. I've always been fascinated by apes, personally. Maybe *terrified* is closer to the truth. I guess ever since I'd read Edgar Allan Poe's "Murders in the Rue Morgue," I figured one day a gorilla or an orangutan might kill me and shove my body up a chimney, like the woman killed by an orangutan in that story.

Mackenzie was checking the safari pants and jacket that had been thrown over a metal chair in the corner. "These must have been his clothes," she said.

"Probably," I said. "Every time I ever saw him on TV he was wearing that kind of getup. Colonel Sanders had his white suits. Ivan had his tailored safari outfits and pith helmets."

"What's with the specks and smears?" Mac asked, checking a splattering of amber streaks and bits of gook that had soiled the clothes. "It looks like the kind of stuff you find on a car if it's parked under the wrong tree."

I checked the spots. "You're right," I said. "They look like sap."

"But sap runs in the spring, not in October."

Whatever, it was pretty clear Ivan Allen wasn't going to pop up like a jack-in-the-box, so we followed the passageway back and left the way we had come in. Just past the sea-lion rookery there was a post with pictures and signs pointing the way to all the exhibits and habitats. The arrow for the Congo had a gimmicky personal ad for a gorilla written on it, no doubt something Ivan had dreamed up: POWERFUL SILVERBACK SEEKS COMPANION FOR MEANINGFUL RELATIONSHIP AND OFFSPRING. ME: 5 FEET, 650 POUNDS; DOMINANT MALE; VEGETARIAN; YOU: FEMININE, FERTILE FEMALE COMFORTABLE WITH GROUP LIVING.

I didn't believe the vegetarian part entirely because I had heard of and read about several pet gorillas that eat chopped meat. There was one I read about that some old woman kept in a cage made of nothing but chicken wire in a bungalow in Houston that ate shell steaks and veal parmigiana. There are exceptions to everything, let me tell you.

Mac and I followed the path that cut a swath down the center of the zoo grounds. We took a shortcut through the elephant and rhino building. It always smells to high heaven in there. But there were a lot of interesting new signs in the stable viewing area. Stuff that interests me I like to repeat over and over until I have it memorized. Such as: "Elephants gather in groups. They constantly talk to and touch each other; led by the oldest and

16

largest cow for life, they can create a complex community." That's the kind of thing I'll think about for weeks, and probably even dream about.

A lot of the facilities had been modernized since Mac and I had been there on our last class trip. There were a lot of pictures of poachers with elephants they'd slaughtered. Included were dozens of gruesome color videos and photos of animals with their heads ripped open and their tusks carved out.

"That is so barbaric," Mac said. "I could just throw up."

"Me, too," I agreed. "And we used to make piano keys out of elephant tusks, too."

We went past the House of Wolves, a first-aid station, and the Dancing Crane Cafe. Most of the stands were closed for the season, but the main zoo store was open. It was filled with things like zebra bookshelves, chairs in the shape of lions, African rattan baskets, and rather macabre stuffed toy animals. The World of Darkness, with vampire bats and other weird nocturnal creatures, sat up on a hill like the house in *Psycho*. Here, the main route dropped sharply to the right and into a bend.

Within a hundred yards Mac and I stood transfixed at the entrance to the Congo Land and the Gorilla Forest, where it seemed we were peering into a frightening manifestation of Ivan Allen's mind. We knew he had been behind the project, that it was the birth of his imagination, this slab of a jungle wall that stood before us. There were lengths of high, strong metal fencing dressed and hidden with impenetrable thickets of African bamboo and vines. Over the clumps of massive real and artificial boulders rose a forest of mangroves, balsa, and mimosa trees, a thousand trunks shooting up over a hundred feet high from a maze of half-buried buttresslike roots. The forest's canopy practically blotted out the sun.

The main gate itself was like the gaping mouth of a monstrous viper with two vast, closed wooden doors that looked like they were holding back a minotaur or King Kong. The whole facade was something huge and secret and frightening. I took a deep breath as the sound of a motor began to intrude.

Mac and I looked up to see a man descending from the canopy toward us like some sort of astronaut with a jet pack.

"Egad," I muttered.

"What is this?" Mackenzie said.

It took a moment before we realized that the floating human form was in some sort of a wire gondola attached to the end of a long hydraulic arm with collapsible sections, like a fishing rod. The base of the arm was the bed of a customized heavy-duty truck.

We watched the man working the control levers in the gondola steer himself out of the jungle. Up close, he looked to be about sixty. He was wearing a groundskeeper's uniform, and had a face like a grouchy, wrinkled pink linen suit. As he floated to within twenty feet of us, what struck me most was that the gondola he was in was covered with the same sort of amber specks we'd seen on Ivan Allen's clothes—and I hadn't seen them anywhere else at the zoo.

"The Congo doesn't open for another hour," the man said. His name tag read: HENNING. He looked like he'd been working hard, to judge from the sweat stains on his shirt and a missing button. A smile broke across his face; he must have thought we were just a couple of regular kids visiting the zoo.

"Will we be able to see the gorillas?" Mac asked. She had let her hair down and shook it loose. She always does that whenever she really wants to disarm somebody. "I love gorillas."

"Sure," the groundskeeper said.

"How about the jaguars?" I said.

"Nope," he replied. The smile faded from his face, but he still looked pretty friendly. "We're working on their moat. You might be able to see them at the end of the day. Maybe tomorrow."

He grasped the gondola's controls and started to guide it away from us and back toward the base of the truck. Mac and I ran after him. "What're all those specks on your bucket?" I called over the whir of the motor. "They look like some kind of sap."

"Yep."

"Our bio and science teachers told us that trees only

have sap in the spring," I said, trying to sound like a really mentally challenged student. Mac did a little skip and let out an inane giggle to help me out. "I don't see any sap on the ground," I added.

The man stopped his gondola right over us. "You get an Indian summer like this one, and the tops of the mangroves and mimosas think it's spring. The canopy gets a lot of sap."

"Only in the canopy?" Mac asked. "Just those top branches of the forest?"

"Yeah," the man said. He looked ready to grasp the controls again, and then stared at us. "Why'd you ask?"

I decided to go for the full shock value. "Her mom's the city medical examiner," I said, indicating Mac. "We were just wondering how all the sap specks and smudges got on Ivan Allen's clothes. Were you around when they found the body?"

The man's face hardened into what looked to me to be a mask of anger and hate. I thought he was going to spit on us, but instead he looked back toward the outer jungle of the Congo, as if we no longer existed. He squeezed the control sticks and the hydraulic crane began to extend, lifting him back over the fence and up toward the treetops. I was going to yell something after him just to make him really nuts, but I heard the sound of sirens as a gaggle of cop cars pulled onto the zoo grounds. Three patrol cars with lights flashing came right down the roadway and into a service road that circled around the back of the Congo complex.

"Something's happened," I said. "Let's get back."

As we hurried up the main path returning the way we'd come, I yanked my cell phone out and punched in Mrs. Riggs's cell number. "What's up, Kim?" I said. She likes Mac's friends to call her Kim, so I do. Mac made me stop near the Dancing Crane Cafe so she could jam her ear next to mine and listen, too.

"We've got a crime scene," Mrs. Riggs said. "You'd better get back here pronto."

"What?" Mac yelled into the receiver.

"What'd you find out about the blood?" I asked. I knew it had to have something to do with that. "It's the blood, right?"

"Yeah," Mrs. Riggs said.

If the zoo had been declared a crime scene, both Mackenzie and I knew what the crime had to be. "You think someone murdered Ivan? Is that what you think now? Someone deliberately gave him the wrong kind of blood?"

"Bingo."

"How do you know it wasn't an accident?" I asked. "Maybe the labels just got mixed up. He was type A. What type did they give him?"

"Gorilla," Mrs. Riggs said, sounding really weirded out.

"Gorilla?" Mac repeated, shocked.

"Yes, nice, *fresh* gorilla blood," Mrs. Riggs clarified.

## 3

### Suspect Behavior

**By the time we got back** to the administration building, I was on automatic, eating a third strip of licorice I had pulled from the catchall left pocket of my jeans. Mac gets chills on the top of her head whenever she senses something isn't quite right, and I get an uncontrollable urge to eat a Clark Bar or a Baby Ruth. Of course, I had to switch to licorice after I read a government report about how every single chocolate bar you buy in a store is permitted to have a minimum of eight insect legs and three rat hairs in it.

As we came around the sea-lion rookery we saw Mrs. Riggs on the steps of the main building firing off orders and pointing toward her van. A couple of men in suits were carrying Ivan's body out on a gurney. They stopped a moment for her to do a last-minute check. Ivan was wrapped up like a mummy in a white sheet, which is what coroners do with celebrities and important people. With a regular person they usually just shove the body into a black rubber bag and close it up like a carrot stick in a Ziploc bag.

Mrs. Riggs gave the guys a final okay and waved them on to the oval, which had filled with a dozen flashing cop and technician cars parked helter-skelter. The man in front of the stretcher reached down, grabbed a leather loop, and began to pull the gizmo along behind him like some kind of freakazoid sled on wheels.

"Hey, Kim, what was with the blood?" I said.

Mrs. Riggs took off her dingy fedora and adjusted the purple-and-red fishing flies that were hooked into its tattered band. The hat had belonged to her dad, who was the most famous and brilliant chief medical examiner New York City had ever had. She had worn the hat all the time since her dad had died a couple of years before, which I thought was weird at first, but I've gotten used to it. People have a right to mourn however they want, if you ask me—but that's another story.

"If a patient can die from getting a transfusion from the wrong type of human blood," Mrs. Riggs said, "you can imagine what happened when they gave Ivan Allen a pint of gorilla blood." She put the hat back on, turned, and headed inside and down the corridor to the hospital wing. "Talk about a wrong agglutinogen—the red blood cells in his veins turned into clumps the size of marbles!"

We trailed her through the mob of police and the forensic technicians who were moving through the facilities like a band of caffeinated locusts.

"Does the zoo have anything other than stored

animal blood at the hospital?" Mackenzie asked.

"Yes," Mrs. Riggs said. "They've got state-of-the-art animal-care facilities on the grounds and more veterinarians than you could hang on a fence. Perry told me the primates have their own vet facilities as part of the Congo compound. Endoscopy, laser surgery, microsurgery, dentistry, radiology: the works."

"It sounds like a Mt. Sinai for monkeys," I said.

"The way he described it, it is."

Mrs. Riggs walked the length of the main lab, which looked like one big crummy white-tiled loft—very much like a couple of the hospitals Mac and I saw in Dublin and the south of France. Some of the antique equipment was kept around like curios in a museum, and you could tell there was no really inspired custodian cleaning the place. The important equipment and areas looked sterile enough, but the windowsills had dust on them and the plants were neglected.

Mackenzie loves plants, so she started plucking off the dead blossoms of a potted geranium that was sitting in over an inch of water. Nobody seemed to care if the pots drained right or not. There was a whole window box of begonias and African violets that were too dry.

"This is pathetic," Mackenzie mumbled as she tried sopping up some of the water from the base of the geranium. I myself was more interested in the more modern gizmos, the several steel tables with microscopes, retorts, and balances in glass cases. The whole whitewashed left wall was mainly marble sinks and work areas with spigots for Bunsen burners and culture incubators. Banks of fluorescent tubes hovered from the ceiling like blazing islands of cruelly bright light.

Mrs. Riggs stopped outside the doorway of the blood storage room. "Whoever killed Ivan Allen had to know how to sedate a gorilla, draw blood, and then get the blood into one of those cold-storage units." She was pointing into the room toward a row of stainless steel cylinders about the size of eighty-gallon water vats. Each one had an elaborate lid with heavy-duty sealing latches and external gauges showing the sub-zero temperatures inside.

The only other furnishing in the room was an aluminum counter with a beaker holding about a dozen cheapo white plastic ballpoints and a single small pencil. A detective and a couple of fingerprint technicians were inching over everything in the room and dusting it with white powder.

Mackenzie and I were trying to take in the circus going on around us. Almost all the crime scenes we've ever seen have been frenzied and crazed when the police first get there.

Mac took a pad and pen out of her purse. She's very good at observing unusual details at a crime scene. She checked out the blood room, and when she was finished peering in there, she focused in on the small hospital staff, headed by a snobby-looking doctor. The police were questioning a tall skinny teenage boy—some kind of zoo candy striper with a long face like a horse, who looked scared to death. There was also a bleach-blond orderly with a name tag that read MAXINE BLESSMAN. She had a build like a weight lifter and looked like she could take Chynna to the mat.

Lieutenant Jamieson, the Bronx detective appointed to the case, came over to Mrs. Riggs. She spoke to him in a tone I've heard her take when she's being careful not to step on anyone's toes. She knew it was politic to let the Bronx crew know she wasn't trying to tell them how to do their job. Jamieson was staring at me and Mac.

"This is my daughter, Mackenzie," Mrs. Riggs told him, "and her pal P.C. They're very much interested in police work."

Lieutenant Jamieson, in his mouse-gray suit and fat brown tie, looked amused for a moment, and then spoke to us. "Great," he said. "It's good to start any career when you're very young."

"Actually, they've already helped in a few murder cases," Mrs. Riggs went on. "They're really very cunning, but maybe a little too dauntless. I guess that runs in the family."

Jamieson looked stumped for a moment. "We've got a lot of New York precincts that could use some fresh young blood."

That last word wasn't out of his mouth before he realized that under the circumstances he might have better chosen some other cliché. The lieutenant looked to be about forty years old, solid like an astronaut, and he had a deep monotone voice like Robocop.

Sergeant Zoode, in police uniform, came out of the blood room and reported to Lieutenant Jamieson. The sergeant was a middle-aged guy with a paunch, and blond hair like a Viking's that burst out from the sides of his cap. He sounded extremely competent and crackerjack. He clutched a clipboard and was scribbling things down even faster than Mac. "There's too much condensation forming and reforming in the blood room. We couldn't lift a single print," Zoode said. "Not even from the pens."

Jamieson turned to Mrs. Riggs. He held the transfusion bag that had contained the gorilla blood. I could see Ivan Allen's name clearly printed on it with an indelible pen. "The transfusion bag came out of the center storage vat. How the gorilla blood even got in there is anyone's guess."

"Anyone who worked here this morning could have made the switch," Sergeant Zoode said. "Anyone else, even someone from another part of the zoo, would have stood out."

"Did any of the other stored bags have Ivan's name on them?"

"No," Zoode said. "Just the one, and we found that one drained and empty, hanging from the intravenous stand."

"Well, I hope you find something useful," Mrs. Riggs said. "I'll get the body downtown and have the preliminary results of the autopsy by tonight. I'm not expecting any more surprises." Mrs. Riggs reached out her hands like the wings of a condor and let one plop on Mackenzie's shoulder and the other on mine. "Let's vamoose, kids."

She tried to turn us away but I didn't move.

"What?" Mrs. Riggs said.

"Can't we stay?" I said, watching the last of the cops and technicians exit the blood room. They began to lock and seal it. "I mean, Mac and I?"

"Stay?" Mac said, looking excited.

Mrs. Riggs saw the glint in our eyes. "Oh, I don't think so," she said.

Perry broke away from the small cluster of hospital staff. "Kim, are you leaving?" he asked.

"Yes." Then she indicated us and added, "But the kids want to know if they can hang out at the zoo for a while."

Lieutenant Jamieson jumped in. "I wouldn't advise that. My men and I have a lot of work to do and they'd"—he considerately switched his attention directly to us—"*you'd* be in the way."

"Excuse me, Lieutenant," I said loudly, "are your men finished in the blood room?"

Jamieson twitched at the volume of my voice. For a moment his lips curled into a sort of sneer, but he noticed everyone in the lab had heard me and was watching for his reaction. Slowly, his lips reformed into a cross between a smile and an expression of confusion. It was as if he were trying to process something he hadn't read in his police procedural manuals.

"Yes, they're finished," he said to me. "We found nothing in there." There was a sternness in his voice now. "Why'd you ask?" he whispered, like I was supposed to answer in kind.

"Because I was wondering why there's that single little pencil in the beaker with the bunch of white ball-points?"

"Yes," Mac added, checking her notes. "The little blue pencil with the words 'Yonkers Raceway' stamped on it in gold."

Everyone turned to look through the glass door of the blood room at the beaker and its contents squatting on the lone table. "Oh, excuse me." Maxine Blessman spoke up, her voice cracking. "I found that pencil on the floor in there this morning."

"After Ivan's death?" Jamieson asked.

"After his *transfusion*?" I said, more to the point.

"Well, yes," the nurse said. "I picked it up automatically, and put it in the beaker with the pens. We keep all the records in ink so I did think it was unusual. You know, we have to note the temperatures every couple of hours. . . . I suppose I'm just a neatness freak, I mean, seeing the pencil on the floor. . . ." She was rambling now. "So . . . I just picked it up and put it in with the pens."

The lieutenant glared at her as if he wanted to choke her. "I guess I should have mentioned it," she said, as a last sputter. "I didn't realize that it might be a *clue*."

"Can we stay in the dorm?" I asked Perry as I took Mackenzie's arm and started escorting her out of the lab. I wasn't even going to wait for another comment from the lieutenant or Sergeant Zoode, because as far as I could see Mac and I were really going to be needed on this case. The zoo's Education Building is right next to the administration building, and I knew they had plenty of rooms for teachers and students to have sleepovers and special instructions during field trips.

"It's all right with me," Perry said, looking to see how this was all sitting with Kim. "I don't know if there's any clean linen. We just had students in from England and Papua New Guinea, and—"

"No problem," I said. "Mac can ride back with Kim and pick up our sleeping bags and toothbrushes and stuff, and bring them out on the subway. I'll stay and get to work."

Mackenzie looked as if she were going to hack my head off, but when I mouthed the words *I SHOPPED FOR THE PICKLE*, all she did was suck in a deep breath of air and swallow. "I mean," I added quickly, "we're going to need our toothbrushes and pj's, too. I'll call my aunt and she'll have everything ready to pick up." My aunt Doris and uncle John live five stories above my dad and me, in an apartment house across from Lincoln Center.

Mac didn't say a word to me as Perry and I walked her and Kim to the van, which already had been loaded with the dead body. Kim kept yakking at me to make certain I really thought it was a good idea for Mac and me to sleep at the zoo. "I mean, sleep here? Sleep? Isn't that a little extreme?"

"I'll watch out for them," Perry assured Kim.

I opened the passenger side door of the coroner's van for Mac to step up and get in, but she turned to me. I couldn't tell if she was going to smack me or just what she was going to do. Her arms shot out suddenly and gripped me. "You be careful until I get back," she said, and she really meant it. "There's a slightly twisted sicko killer running around this zoo. And I've got chills on the top of my head big time."

"Hurry back," I said, laughing.

I waited until the van had driven out of sight before I jammed my hand into my jean pocket for a double stick of licorice.

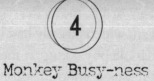

# 4

## Monkey Busy-ness

**"I was very impressed with the way** you noticed that pencil in the blood room," Perry said as I walked with him back toward the administration building.

"That's the kind of thing Mac and I do," I said. "We catch the off-the-wall stuff that the cops and detectives miss or don't figure out on the first go-around. Of course, we do stuff that'd make regular cops shake in their boots. We've got advantages over them."

"Advantages?"

"Sure. Mac and I don't have to read anyone their Miranda rights. She and I don't have to get search warrants or have to worry about entrapment laws."

"I never thought of it quite like that," Perry said, "but I suppose you don't."

"Killers know that half the time cops have their hands tied behind their backs. Mac and I can be more creative. We can make mistakes and nobody sues us. We'll do anything and everything to catch a criminal. You know as well as I do that if the cops don't come up with a hot lead in twenty-four hours—at best, forty-eight—that the case is never going to be solved. Most killers get away with murder, and everybody knows it! Of course, there's a downside to being an amateur."

"I'm sure. . . ."

"Yeah," I said. "Sometimes we end up alone with an armed maniac and almost get *ourselves* killed."

Perry stopped and stared at me with shock, until I let out a big laugh.

"Only kidding," I said. But I really wasn't.

I hit Perry with a few questions while I had the chance. "Did Ivan have a lot of enemies outside the zoo?" I asked. "From seeing him on TV, I'd say he looked like the kind of guy people would line up to hate. At least, to me."

Perry smoothed back his elegant, razor-cut gray hair and got that kind of phony look in his eyes I usually see politicians get when they're marching in things like the St. Patrick's Day parade. "His public persona was very much loved, which is why he was so good at fund-raising," he said, choosing his words like a man selecting pears at a fruit market. "He didn't have much family he ever talked about. Maybe a cousin or two back in Germany. He emigrated years ago. . . ."

"Who despised him most around here?" I said.

"I wouldn't use the word 'despise,'" Perry said, lowering his voice. "There were many of his colleagues who were jealous of his celebrity, but . . ." Just the way he said that, I could tell there were probably dozens of workers who detested Ivan, which is what I figured. Perry's mind sidestepped and then tripped over something. "You know, there is something. He used to get anonymous notes. I mean, he got them over the years, as far as I could see. He told me he had gotten maybe a dozen. Notes that always said the same thing. I saw a couple of them—they were each printed in charcoal—thick charcoal, block letters on various kinds of ordinary paper. Yellow legal paper. Pieces of paper bag. Scraps of anything. They all said the same thing: 'Remember Paterfamilias.'"

"Who or what is Paterfamilias?"

"I don't know—and Ivan never wanted to talk about it. But the notes were very disturbing to him." Perry looked up thoughtfully. "Whenever I was around and he opened one, well, his reaction was the same as others on the staff had told me. The blood would drain from his face, and he'd punch something. Slam his fist down on a table or against a wall. He said he didn't know what the notes meant, but I think he did."

"Oh, and there were fires lately," Perry added. "I meant to remind the police about those. They'd have them on record."

"Fires?"

"Yes, little ones, like brush fires just outside the zoo grounds. One time someone had set a couple of old tires burning. You know, all that smoke. The first one was a couple of months ago on the other side of the Bronx River. We've only got a few Sambar deer, elk, and herons there now, but I remember Ivan got a note right after that."

"Did they find who set the fires?"

"It looked like kids," Perry said. "We've got a couple of rough schools in the area, and a lot of low-income housing. Poor kids. Neglected kids. There was a second brush fire on the Bronx Park South boundary of the zoo near the Red River hogs, and just last week there were two incidents near Grote Street. It seemed like Ivan got notes after each of those, now that I think of it. . . ."

He looked at me to see if there was anything else I wanted to ask, but I really needed to get to work and start checking things out.

"You know, P.C.," Perry said, and for once he seemed to speak from the heart. "I've been able to get the cooperation of everyone to keep the murder out of the press until Monday. The press already knows Ivan died. It'll be in the afternoon *Post* and all over the TV news tonight. But there is an extremely important meeting of the Wildlife Association and our biggest corporate contributors on Tuesday. It's a very critical lunch in terms of the zoo's budget. We were putting our best foot forward. Our whole facilities here—the animals!—everything we've been building toward depends upon their complete and utter support. They will be shocked enough to hear of Ivan's death as an accident, but I think an unsolved murder would make things impossible around here."

"Things like funds for the panda project?" I said.

"Yes. I might be able to swing their emotions into making it a memorial for Ivan, but not if there's still all this mystery and dread about a murderer stalking among us. Nobody's going to write a check with that hanging in the air."

"What are you saying?"

"Just that anything you and Mackenzie can do to help the police catch this killer as soon as possible will be very appreciated. I know you must think I sound cold-blooded about this, but I care very much about what happens to the animals."

*Yes, you're worried about the animals and about keeping your own job*, I felt like saying. Instead I said, "We'll try our best." I quizzed Perry on a couple of things about the hospital staff, and told him to get the word out that Mac and I would be poking around the place.

"Of course," he said. "I'll call the departments and see that you have access."

"Especially to the Congo area and to Ivan's office and files," I said. "I'm going to want to see what kind of stuff he's left on his computer. That sort of thing."

Perry agreed, but I could tell that he wasn't really bubbling with confidence over our taking on the case. I let him go back to the cops, but I took off around the sea lions and headed down past the rhinos and elephants. Three giraffe heads peered at me from the tops of enormous stable doors. I wanted to keep out of Lieutenant Jamieson's way for a while, and I'd already formed an initial impression of the weirdos at the hospital who could have switched the transfusion bags:

1. The trainee kid's name was Peter Sandusky, Perry had told me. From the brief glimpse I'd gotten of him at the hospital, he looked scared and fragile. My guess was that he was a real social-loser type, and Perry told me he went to the Bronx High School of Science, which I hear is Nerd Nirvana. This also meant that he was probably pretty smart.

2. I certainly counted Maxine Blessman out, because if she had been the killer, I didn't think she would have admitted picking up the racing pencil from the floor and putting it in the beaker—unless she was much, much cleverer than she seemed—and I doubted that. I bet the only law she broke was probably the one against swigging steroids—but who knew?

3. That left only the doctor. He didn't seem like he'd be capable of plotting much more than how to slip hot peppers into a Philly cheese-steak recipe. Perry told me he was from Pakistan and that his name was Mohammed Jahangir. He looked neurotic and inexperienced, but he was apparently the best physician the zoo could afford. There was a lot more for me to check out before I started to speculate too much about anyone or anything.

More important than the blood switcheroo, and at the top of my curiosity list, was finding out who at that zoo had the opportunity and know-how to jab a gorilla with a hypo and drain out a pint of its fresh blood without being bitten or killed. Apes and monkeys at any age can really bite!

As I walked, I yanked my cell phone out of my pocket and tried to call Mac and my pal Jesus Lopez. Jesus is only thirteen years old, but he's been a computer maestro for years. I knew he'd salivate at the challenge of running through the zoo's database to check for anything fishy. Codes or no codes, Jesus could hack his way into the Chinese equivalent of the Pentagon, if he had to. The phone rang a half dozen times before his voice mail came on, but I didn't leave a message.

While I had the phone out I touched base with my aunt Doris. I told her to please go down to my and my dad's apartment, put some stuff in a bag, and give Mackenzie my backpack when she swung by.

It took me a good ten minutes to get as far as the World of Darkness. As the main road dropped to the right and into its bend, I kept my gaze up toward the jungle canopy for the freaky groundskeeper in his sap-stained basket, but he was nowhere in sight. The crane truck itself was parked in the zoo's vehicle area, and just beyond, the massive entrance doors to the Congo Gorilla Forest attraction were wide open.

I passed through the entryway of towering bamboo and thick vines that hung down like twisted tentacles toward the dark canopy. The route narrowed into a passageway that wove its way by the huge real and cement rocks and giant mangrove roots. In places there were tunnels, one of which passed right through the middle of several of the huge trees. There was a stretch where the side of the labyrinth was nothing more than a fence along the edge of a moat.

There were several policemen and technicians in line moving slowly across an open savanna terrain. I figured this had to be the jaguar area. A cluster of technicians on their hands and knees had to mark the spot where the wounded Ivan had been found. There were screams of jaguars coming from my right, and I glimpsed the big cats snarling from behind the gates of their indoor enclosure. A couple of zoo workers in white smocks were busy talking to the cops.

I moved onward past a few interactive gizmos for the public to play with, like a measuring stick to check the size of elephant footprints. Then the sign said if you multiply that figure by six you get the height of a forest elephant. And there was a whole radio-transmitter tracking device—part of the jaguar exhibit. You could swivel the transmitter until its beeping sound showed you had zeroed in on one of the jaguars' radio collars. The sign said all six of the jaguars had been outfitted with the devices, and kids were challenged to try to locate all six in the paddock. There was a lot of kid stuff like that where the tunnel became completely glass.

Animals were feeding and lurking and stalking just behind the glass, and it was as if you were right in the middle of them. There were mandrills, guenons, several okapis—which look like a weird cross between a zebra and a little giraffe—and lots of hornbills, gibbons, and clusters of Goliath beetles, the largest beetles in the world. There was nothing between me and them except this thick, bulletproof kind of glass.

The see-through tunnel curved and I had to pass through a revolving-door climate seal. A wave of warm, humid air rushed over me as the incredible glass tunnel curved again and again, until I could see that it ended in a steel-and-glass structure that looked like a huge mother ship out of *Battlestar Galactica*.

Speakers brought the sounds of the jungle inside, and once I was in the main structure itself, I crossed a bridge over a stream. I soon found myself in a vast octagonal room, each of the four sides to my left made of floor-to-ceiling glass. Behind the glass were a half dozen gorillas staring at me from an indoor African habitat.

A striking woman in a big, stiff brown wig and a white clingy skirt and jacket turned away from the glass, locked on a huge toothy smile, and came gliding across the room toward me. "You must be P.C.," she said, like a wanna-be vampire in polyester. "What a handsome young detective. I've been waiting for you."

**5**

## Gargantua

**"I'm Dr. Betty Waters," the woman said**. "Perry asked me to watch out for you."

Betty smoothed her shiny uniform, and reformed her expression into one that was even more glamorously pretentious. She looked to be in her early forties, and her face was so thick with chalk-white makeup that she looked like a mime. Her scarlet lips were puffy, like people who have had collagen shots to look more lusciouslipped, and her black eyebrows were arched so high they looked as if you could drive a Honda Civic under them. I couldn't wait until Mac could get a load of her.

"I guess Perry thought I'd be the most helpful," she said. "He warned me that you were a very talented teenage investigator and that you'd be asking a lot of questions." Her tone was playful, as if she were addressing a slightly naughty idiot child. I decided to let her think that for a while.

"Did you work with Ivan Allen?" I asked.

"Not really. I mean, I wasn't under his direct

supervision," she said. "I'm in charge of the chimpanzee breeding program—a whole other ball of wax."

"I guess it would be."

"Yes," she said. "The adult chimps are so aggressive we often have to keep the babies in our nursery a good deal longer than the gorillas' offspring. We've had cases where the male chimps will try to devour their own offspring, but, thank God, that's the exception."

"That's horrible."

"Yes, it is." Betty reached her rather delicate, long arms up to smooth her hair—well, her dirt-colored wig. It was really an el cheapo—it looked as if she'd break her hair if she fell down. And you could tell she wasn't wearing it as a disguise, but as a proud fashion statement she'd come across on the Shopping Channel. Actually, the wig was more than a statement: it was a scream.

"Have you seen our gorilla family before?" she said, turning and clip-clopping back in her unsensible shoes toward the slabs of glass. "Perry says you've been here a number of times with your school—and he said something about your father working at the Museum of Natural History?"

"Right," I said. "But I haven't been to the zoo since you built the Congo." I made my eyes bulge so she'd think I was even more of a fool than she already did. "It's quite impressive. I suppose there are several zoologists who work here. I mean, ones who worked closely with Ivan."

"Oh, yes," Betty said. "Of course, most of them

weren't working last night, but the police are putting them through their paces now in the jaguar enclosure—you know, where they found Dr. Allen after the attack. They're going over everything with a fine-toothed comb."

"Did they find anything unusual?"

"From what I've heard, the answer is yes and no. There were a couple of foreign coins, at least that's what a cage cleaner told me. They had him out there with them raking. All the custodians around here are terrible gossips, you know. I personally don't think that's very weird, about the coins, because one of our vets, Dr. Lumet—he's from Dijon, France, where they make the mustard—well, I believe the coins were French, and he's always flying there to see his mother. I believe he has a Dijon significant other there, too. Whatever, he's always complaining how the banks and currency mobiles at the airports will only change back paper money."

"That's happened to me when I've traveled in Europe, too," I said.

Betty paused, as though she had to process the fact that I had actually traveled once in a while myself. "Yes," she forged on, "Dr. Lumet gets stuck with a lot of foreign coins and always tries to shove them into our Coke machines like slugs. He ends up jamming all the snack machines."

"Was he on duty last night?"

"No," Betty said. "At least, he wasn't scheduled. As far

as I knew, only Ivan and a couple of assistants were here. Well, actually, they said Lumet was here for a while, but I guess it's no secret he likes his wine. . . . Of course, I know the police are going to want alibis for all of us, but I don't think Lumet would kill anyone, although—"

"Were you here last night?" I asked.

"I've been in the Congo every night for the last three weeks, in the breeding annex," she said. "One of our chimps gave birth to a premature baby, so I've had to stay to check the incubator every couple of hours. The baby's doing fine—but what I was about to say is that several workers at the zoo like a nip or two, though I suppose Franchot—that's Dr. Lumet—liked his wine more than some. But do I think he murdered Ivan? No, of course not. Franchot isn't capable of that. I mean, that's just my opinion. I happen to have a theory of my own."

I could see that she loved to babble. "Like what?'

"Well, I think this whole blood thing was some sort of crazy, accidental mix-up."

"A blood mix-up?"

As Betty and I stood in front of the wall of glass, the entire gorilla family stared at us. One ape was sitting right down front on a log, with a couple of others just behind her. Several more were scattered across higher elevations in the habitat, and a few were just sleeping.

"Precisely," she said. "Ivan was always doing exactly what he wanted around here. He could very easily have taken blood from one of the gorillas and brought it up to the hospital around the same time he was donating his own blood and—well, Ivan was brilliant, but he often forgot what he was doing. He probably mixed the blood up himself, he was such a control freak—shoved the wrong bag of blood into the wrong place, and—I mean, Lord only knows.

"We don't pay our workers very much. Half of them can't speak English. And besides, with help the way it is now I can't even drive into Micky D's and be certain I'm going to come out the other end with my sausage McMuffin or a complete Happy Meal. They're always leaving out the Diet Coke or the ketchup packets or something. I'm just saying it could have been truly an accident—that's my personal hypothesis."

Betty noticed I was staring with terror at the biggest gorilla that lurked halfway up the landscape near a curtain of vines. He was staring at me as though I were a threat to his whole family, and looked like he might at any moment charge straight at me, shatter the glass, and bite my throat.

"That's our silverback," Betty said. "Gargantua. Ivan named him after the famous gorilla P. T. Barnum had at his circus over a half century ago. And, of course, Barnum stole the name from the big fat king who loved food and drink—you know, the one Rabelais wrote about. Whatever, our Gargantua is a very good daddy to his babies. Always has been. He's nine years old and weighs over a quarter of a ton. Just loves to play with his kids."

"He doesn't seem to like my talking to you," I said.

"Oh, don't be insulted. He's jealous of any male he sees me with," she said. "He knows I'm the only one around here who really looks after him. He loves me to talk to him and spend time with him—behind the glass, of course. There are a couple of other local women from the housing complex he likes, too. He's got a few other regulars who come to the zoo week after week just to see him." She laughed. "All the gorillas love visitors."

She moved along the glass wall to where another gorilla was holding a baby that looked as if it had drunk a few too many tequila sunrises.

"This is the largest female, called Mama. She's the wife of Gargantua and the mother of their four-month-old son, Elf. We call the baby that because of his pointed ears, of course." Betty pointed up to the left of the habitat. "The adult female sitting on the slate rise is Auntie. Sometimes we call her 'Hear No Evil' because she has this habit of putting her hands over her ears. She's related to one old female that was here at the zoo many years ago that used to do the same thing. The two gorillas had never met, so we've really had to wonder if the behavior was genetically based."

There were signs and explanations of which one each of the gorillas was so all the visitors could figure every-thing out on their own. In the back was Jimbo, an uncle to Elf. And there were a couple of other aunts and a few two-year-olds. "The aunts all help Mama with the baby-sitting, but Gargantua does his share of entertaining and teaching his son. They're really all one big happy gorilla family."

Betty did a turn almost like a little dance step, and swallowed me with another of her enormous smiles. I could see she still thought I was a pubescent cretin, so I thought it was about time I showed my true colors.

"Which gorilla did Ivan's killer get the blood from?"

Betty lifted her left eyebrow further, if that was possible. She was definitely taking a closer look at me. "I noticed a smear of blood on Gargantua's fur at the crook of his left arm, so it would seem the blood that killed Ivan came from him."

"Do they take blood out of gorillas a lot around here?"

"Once in a while," Betty said. "Cornell and Columbia—a couple of other universities, too—pester us a few times a year for primate blood. They donate money, so we're supposed to jump every time their vet school needs a sample for their students to study."

"Is there any record of anyone taking blood last night?"

"Well, no—but Ivan didn't always tell everyone what he was ordering or doing. If someone offered him money, he'd stick the gorillas as if they were pincushions."

"But how is it done—I mean, actually?"

Betty led the way through a pair of black metal

swinging doors on which was written STAFF ONLY in large orange letters. There were several other windows on the gorilla's indoor habitat, and a thick glass door, which led into a chamber that looked like the kind they stick quiz-show contestants in when they're not supposed to hear anything.

"This is the holding room," Betty said. "We would sequester the gorilla we wanted to treat in here. Let's just say whoever takes blood out of a gorilla would have needed to know what he was doing. Any one of the zoologists, or one of the animal handlers, could easily coax Gargantua out of the main habitat and into the holding chamber. All the gorillas relate to the workers here—and they each knew Ivan very well—but a number of others could have accomplished the isolation of a gorilla."

"And then what?"

"I've seen them sedate Gargantua for dental work and regular health exams. If it was a procedure where the staff had to physically handle the animal, they would fire a drug dart into the gorilla's neck, and it wouldn't take long—a matter of minutes—before the animal would lose consciousness. A zoologist could go in and give medicine or draw blood or anything uncomplicated like that. When they were finished they'd let the animal come to, or administer an antidote to speed up the process.

"If it were something more serious—an operation—

they'd put him out and keep him anesthetized, then bring him into the surgery facility here—like with the tooth extraction. Gorilla medicine is very much like human medicine, of course."

I peered in through one of the viewing windows in the sides of the holding tank. I saw something shiny.

"What's that?" I asked.

"Where?"

I pointed. "There?"

Betty pressed the code into the lock to open the door. She went in, picked the object up, and brought it out. The door locked automatically behind her. "It's another foreign coin," she said, looking very disturbed by it. "I don't know what it was doing in there. Dr. Lumet wasn't scheduled for any procedures that would have required the room."

I turned the coin in my hand. It had a design of olive branches and the profile of a general on it. The denomination was clear. "It's five francs," I said.

"Let me see," Betty said. She checked it and nodded. "You're right."

"Worth about a dollar," I said.

"Is it?"

I placed the coin back into her hand. "I suppose you should give it to the police," I said.

"Yes, I can tell them to add it to the rest of their coin collection for the day."

"Yeah."

She lead me back out through the swinging doors and deposited me in the main public viewing area once more. She glanced at her watch. "Oh, P.C., I'm afraid I don't have any more time just now," she said. "I have to get back to the nursery, and I hope I've been of some help. I imagine you'll be able to turn your visit into some sort of school project or whatever, but I wish you the best of luck." She extended her hand to shake mine, and gave me another of her gigantic smiles. A big kiss-off.

This time the smile was more of a grin and was so fake I decided not to be Mr. Nice Guy anymore. "Just a couple more questions," I said.

"Yes?"

"I was wondering about that weird guy who floats around here in the gondola," I said. "You know, the groundskeeper who seems to be assigned to this area."

"I'm sorry," she said. "I think I know who you're talking about but I hardly know the man."

"Did he have any grudge against Ivan Allen?" I asked bluntly. "My partner and I were talking to him before, and he just clammed up and flew away from us in his bucket. Do you have any idea why he'd do that? Ivan had amber specks all over his clothes, like something from a tree. Maybe you know how they got there?"

She looked at me as if I were a bug that had just bitten her. "Well, no. No, I don't. Ivan was found in the jungle here at the Congo, of course. Found on the ground."

"There's nothing like it on the ground," I said. "No amber spots or specks or anything. The guy in the gondola said that kind of stuff is only found in the canopy at this time. Caused by some kind of false springtime. What would Ivan be doing a hundred feet up in the treetops?"

"The canopy is only fifty feet up," she said.

"Whatever."

She glanced at her watch, and starting heading back through the swinging doors. "I'm sorry," she said, "but I've got to go."

"But could I ask you one last question?" I shot at her fast as a machine gun. "I suppose you might say it's personal."

"*What is it?*"

"Did you take a vacation this year?"

She looked as if she wanted to kick me, so I shot her another quickie. "And where did you go? I mean, I was just wondering."

Her eyes were locked on me now. For a moment she looked like someone who was playing chess and had just had her queen assassinated. She didn't speak while her mind was computing.

"You probably don't remember," I said. "That's okay. Perry will probably know. He's good at all that kind of stuff. Lots of people never remember where they go."

Waters remained frozen for another second, and then a bountiful graciousness rushed back into her face and voice. She smiled at me now as if I were starring in the cast of *Dumb and Dumber* and she were an astonishingly charitable Miss Universe contestant.

"The Dordogne," Betty said.

"The Dordogne?" I repeated, trying to remember where that was—and then it came to me. "Oh, southwest of Paris," I said, "where some kids found all those ancient caves with prehistoric drawings on them."

"Yes," she said. "I was in Milan and San Sebastian, too—but I spent most of my vacation in France." Her upper lip twitched as she backed out of sight through the swinging doors and was gone.

## 6

### An Embarrassment of Hitches

**By a quarter after one I had finished** my preliminary snooping and had quizzed Perry and Lieutenant Jamieson about a few more things I needed to know. I was heading by the tapirs and a see-through, prairie-dog mound when something started wiggling in my pocket. My instantaneous thought was that it was an escaped tarantula, but then I realized I'd forgotten that I'd set my cell phone on *vibrate*. I grabbed it out and punched the answer button.

"I'm getting out of the subway," I heard Mackenzie's excited voice say. "You could come help me, you know!"

"Okay," I said. "I'll meet you."

I knew exactly where the Bronx Zoo's main subway entrance was from my dozen other visits there, so I took off past the zoo classroom buildings and the wild horses' paddock to the Southern Boulevard Gate. I informed the ticket taker, an old lady who looked like Quasimodo in a dress made of chicken-feed bags, that I was a friend of Perry's, then pushed on the revolving bars of the exit-door-thingamajig. I wanted the ticket-taker to get used to the idea that Mackenzie and I might be going in and out a lot.

I got to the mouth of the subway just as Mac was struggling up. She looked like an employee of the Starving Students Moving Company. I grabbed my backpack and sleeping bag and a Zabar's shopping bag she was lugging. She was still half-buried in her own stuff; all I could see was a pair of cat's-eye sunglasses wedged onto the top of her head and her long hair hanging down her back like glistening linguini.

"Did I miss anything?" Mackenzie shot at me immediately. That's what I really like about her: whenever I'm a little whacked out or confused at any point on a case, she jumps in like a rush of adrenaline and gets us going again.

"Egad, I'm on overload," I said, as I gave Quasimodo a wave and marched Mackenzie back into the zoo. The whole way walking back and then some to the dormitory on Astor Court, I brought her up to speed on everything that I'd done and found out while she was getting our stuff.

"That's a good start," she said. "I called Jesus—"

"I tried to get him on my cell."

"—and I told him to stand by because we'd probably need him."

"You can say that again."

The dorm was next to the administration building, and Perry had given me several keys. The main one opened the downstairs door, and then he'd given us a choice of three or four rooms on the second floor.

"This place is deserted," Mackenzie said, her retro platform shoes thumping on the tile floor.

"Perry said there's a night watchman who checks the place," I said. "And they're hoping to turn on the electricity for the building before tonight. They always shut it off between the visits from foreign students to save money. He said there's a lot of light spill from the courtyard anyway, so there shouldn't be any problem.

"Oh, *nice*."

All three of the rooms looked out over the Aquatic Birdhouse and Pond. To the right of those areas was a pen of cassowaries and an entire colony of penguins. Whatever, they all made a terrible racket. We picked the biggest room, which was right next to the floor's unisex bathroom. The bathroom itself was huge, with about a dozen old-fashioned sinks, primitive shower stalls, and long warped metal mirrors everywhere.

Mac dropped her sleeping bag on one side of our dorm room and rolled it out. She always uses one with big dancing Mickey and Minnie Mouses all over it. I rolled mine out, too, near the other wall. It's a plain canvas one that looks like the kind some paratrooper from *Predator* would use.

I never put a sleeping bag against a wall or sit in a restaurant booth against a wall because most bugs come out of the sides and ceilings of a room and come straight down the wall. I've seen so many cockroaches scooting down the sides of New York City dining establishments, it would make you gag.

It was no big deal for the two of us to share the room. That's how Mac and I are accustomed to sleeping whenever we travel with my dad on one of his archaeological digs for the museum. Kim and Dr. Riggs often take us with them on their vacations, too. Since Dr. Riggs is a well-known psychiatrist, he sometimes lets us go along on some of his tax-deductible jaunts to shrink seminars in exotic cities such as Hong Kong and Peoria, Illinois.

I put on one of the clean pullovers my Aunt Doris had sent along with my other stuff. I had started a collection of T's and sweats with Shakespearean insults on them. This one I found at a Greenwich Village street stand, and it had in big scarlet letters on the front: YOU SCULLION! YOU RAMPALLIAN! YOU FUSTILARIAN! I'LL TICKLE YOUR CATASTROPHE!

"Let's talk while we eat," Mac said, slipping on her favorite shoulder bag, which happens to be a three-dollar, fake-leopard-skin statement she'd found in another of her favorite thrift boutiques. "I thought this would be appropriate for the zoo."

I picked up the Zabar's bag and we headed out to the Flamingo pub. We bought Cokes and sat on one of the benches smack in front of the Birds of Prey cages. A mob of jumbo eagles, hawks, and owls seemed to be looking at us as we devoured our lean pastrami sandwiches and wedges of Brie. There were signs all around us with all the grisly details about how these birds' beaks can tear flesh, how their talons can crush a pet cat, and how lots of raptor birds have a high density of sensitive rods in their eyes. That's so they can spot a scampering rodent from seven hundred feet in the air, swoop down, and begin immediately devouring it, in order to regurgitate it for their babies the minute they get back to the nest.

"All right," Mackenzie said, between munches. "I'll tell you what's penetrated my noggin so far. . . ."

We often do that on a case, just tell each other what we think we know. We've got writers in my building who have told me they're always calling each other and telling and retelling each other their plots until they get them straight. Mac and I find that works well for murder cases, too.

"Let's see," Mac said. "In the clue department we have a Yonkers Racetrack pencil, a few French coins, and a bunch of sap stains on Ivan's clothes."

"Right."

"In the freakazoid suspect category, we've got a mess of oddities in a few locations. The hospital and blood room has Mohammed Jahangir, the Pakistani doctor, Maxine Blessman, the lady orderly with the biceps, and—what did Perry tell you was the name of the trembling kid candy striper?"

"Peter Sandusky."

"Got it." Mac took out her pad now and added to her

notes as she talked. "Out at the Congo, we've got the nasty groundskeeper who flies around pruning the canopy in his sap-stained bucket—"

"John Henning."

"Good. And there's Dr. Betty Waters, the zoologist— who, according to your description looks like a slinking stunt puppet from *The Dark Crystal*—and who went to France for her vacation and could have gotten French coins whenever she wanted, anyway. And then, Dr. Franchot Lumet, the vet, with the significant other lover in the town where they make the mustard—and he stuffs francs in the Coke machines. . . . And you said there's a half dozen other workers out there at the lab, and custodians, and, you know from experience, we can't rule out any of the guys at the top, including Perry—I mean, we really shouldn't."

"So what do you think?"

"Two things," Mackenzie said, jumping up, grabbing all our garbage and dumping it in a trash can that was shaped like a hippo. "One, let's go over the time line. And two, let's do that while we get over to the hospital before the cops let Mohammed and the others go."

We had to circle around back past the tapirs and the Monkey House to get to the stairs up from our little valley to Astor Court. Mac kept making notes as we walked.

"Perry said Ivan died at the hospital at exactly seven-forty-eight this morning," I said. "Perry was right there, so I'm sure even your mom's accepting that as gospel.

From checking with Lieutenant Jamieson and what I've pieced together out at the Congo, someone had to make certain—or this part could have been an accident—somehow Ivan had gotten sugar into his system and passed out. You know, had one of his narcoleptic fits around six A.M."

"He could have died from the sugar, you know," Mac said. "But he didn't."

"No," I said. "Ivan's diabetes wasn't that bad, apparently. His little passing-out episode couldn't have lasted much more than a half hour. So he collapsed, went to sleep—whatever you want to call it. . . ."

"How'd he get the sap stains on him?"

"Not from hanging out up in the canopy, as far as I can see," I said. "According to a lot of the staff I've talked to out at the Congo and Gorilla Forest, Ivan hasn't been up a tree in years. What I think is that when Ivan was unconscious, somewhere between six and six-thirty, someone put him in the crane bucket—the one with all the sap on it. Anyone could have been driving the thing, but Ivan was put in that and lifted into the outdoor section of the jaguar habitat. I was talking to one of the workers out there and he said the gates that kept the jaguars indoors for the night are all on computer. The gates open automatically at six-thirty every morning, so that's precisely when the killer wanted Ivan's sleeping body waiting for them."

Mac stopped at the low wall around the sea-lion

rookery and used it as a desktop to scribble a few more sentences. "Then the jaguars come out and one of them starts nibbling at Ivan's throat—"

"But it doesn't kill him, which is why one of the other Congo workers found Ivan alive about six-forty-five. By seven they had Ivan out of the jaguar habitat and raced him up to the hospital in the bed of a plant truck. They woke up Dr. Jahangir in the staff quarters and Perry got there as they were giving Ivan the transfusion—just after seven-thirty—and in fifteen minutes Ivan was dead from the coagulating effect of the gorilla blood."

Mac was up and running again with me after her. Half the cop cars and emergency vehicles were gone from the circle, and by the time we got through the lobby of the administration building and into the waiting room for the hospital annex, Peter Sandusky was gone. Lieutenant Jamieson was just finishing up with Maxine Blessmen, and Doc Jahangir was still being questioned in a corner of the main room.

"Excuse me, Ms. Blessman," Mac said, stopping her as she headed past us. "We were wondering about that pencil you had picked up in the blood room this morning."

"What about it?" Maxine Blessman said, in a tone that suggested she wanted to karate kick the two of us. "You know, I'm tired and I want to go home! I told the cops it was no big thing finding a racetrack pencil. Those pencils are all over this place."

"How come?" Mac asked.

"Look," Ms. Blessman said, starting to flex her arms and automatically do abbreviated limbering-up exercises by holding the side of a doorway. Mac and I see runners stopping and doing exercises like it all the time in Central Park, but I guessed the kind Blessman was doing was more like what weight lifters do. "Dr. Jahangir lives at Yonkers Raceway. They give him a free pencil every time he buys a program. He's there a half dozen times a week. It's nobody's business how he wants to throw around his money. I just had never seen one of the pencils in the blood room before."

"So why this morning?" I said.

"So the doc was in there, was all I figured. Of course, he never *does* goes in there, usually. He does what he's supposed to do, which is practically nothing around this tomb but nap and handicap trotters. You know, he's the great important guy with the M.D. degree. He doesn't do menial work, so it's usually just Peter or me who handles things in the blood room and just about anywhere else around the hospital."

"Peter Sandusky?" Mac said.

"Not Peter Rabbit." Ms. Blessman burped. I noticed for the first time the thickness of the hair that grew from her very narrow brow. The hair burst upward from roots less than an inch and a half above her eyebrows with the coarseness of an albino Neanderthal's. She looked ready to spit at us. "Look,

I'm outta here," she snapped and marched out the door. Mackenzie and I kept our eye on her until we saw her unlock a Harley Davidson and take off around the circle.

"So now we wait for the cops to finish with Mohammed?" Mac muttered.

I turned back to watch the cops working him over. He was gesticulating like crazy and showing them Yonkers Raceway programs. "Let's not," I said. "We'll get to the doc later."

"Then who's next? The nerd?"

"Yep," I said. "I found out he lives right around here, and I've got a strong hunch that as far as the hospital suspects go, we're going to find that good ol' Pete might end up as our top man on the 'quote 'em' pole. Besides, doesn't it bother you that right off the bat the cops have found at least a Yonkers Racetrack pencil and *three* French coins? It seems to me there might be too many clues lying around pointing in the wrong directions."

"Ah, *exactement*," Mac said.

## 7

### Phantom

**Mac and I walked past a border** of lilies of the Nile that surrounded the zoo's main outdoor aviary—a bubble about the size of an inflatable tennis court. We left via one of the exits that was marked PEDESTRIANS ONLY and started making our way along Bronx Park South toward the address Perry had given me for Sandusky.

The first section of Bronx Park South was a quiet residential street like one you might find in Topeka, Kansas. Yet just to our right was the twelve-foot-high brick wall of the zoo, behind which were lots of the animals that our ancestors used to hunt—and the beasts that hunted them all. There were peekaboo spaces between some of the gates in the wall where we could see zebras and peacocks. Some of the more dangerous animals were trapped beyond the wall by deep moats and extra-high electrified fences. A few lions were lying around, sleeping on rocks in the midafternoon sun. Others were pacing as if they were biding their time for the chance to leap from their confines and run the streets.

The row of normal-looking split-level ranch houses on half acres slowly became a more crowded motley collection of frame houses as we turned onto Grote Street. It was as if all zoning laws had stopped. There would be a pizza joint and then a dilapidated Victorian house, and next to that a dry-cleaning store and five more semidetached junky domiciles. Several of the houses with holes in their roofs and boarded-up windows were clearly abandoned. One of the houses that had people still living in it had three feet of prairie grass growing all around it.

"Do you think they're trying to start their own Wild Safari Country?" I said to Mac.

"Are you kidding?" she said. "If I lived here I wouldn't cut my grass either. Say the security breaks down and lots of the zoo animals jump the fence. Where are all the cute tufted deer and gazelles going to go? To my lawn."

"So?" I said. "Then how long do you think it'd take for the carnivores to come a-calling? Your house would become kill-zone central."

"Great," Mackenzie said. "It'll be like Treetops, that hotel in the Africa."

"I can see you sitting at a cash register at the front desk until the first tiger knocks down your front door and drags you off screaming. Tigers still eat sixty people a year in India. Of course, the good news is that figure's down from the annual thousand they used to devour twenty years ago."

Mac ducked out into the street to check the street number on the curb. "Five-oh-one—we're getting close," she said. "I bet the house is right at the end of the block."

"Did you see that shoe commercial about this guy jogging during the Apocalypse?"

"No," Mac said, slowing down her pace. Now each house looked eerier than the next. "I would have remembered that one—and I don't even want to hear about it now, if you don't mind."

Suddenly, out of nowhere, a yellow pinstriped Grand Am screeched down the street and flew into the driveway just a few feet in front of us. I yanked Mac back so she wouldn't get hit.

The car stopped at the end of the driveway. A jumbo-sized mother got out of the car with a couple of young no-neck monsters and about ten Toys "R" Us bags.

"You drive crazy!" Mac blurted out. The woman snarled and disappeared inside her freaky, dumpy house.

I grabbed Mac's elbow again. "This is it."

Mac followed my eye to the gate of the house next to the Twisted Metal mom: 573 and SANDUSKY were legible on the crooked white picket fence.

"Jackpot," Mac said.

As I opened the front gate, I felt something wet on my hand. I pulled back to find my palm and fingers covered with white paint. Not just that water-soluble stuff. This was thick, one-coat gook.

Mac laughed and gave me a Kleenex from her fake-leopard bag, but the paint was so icky the Kleenex, too, stuck to my fingers.

We heard hammering coming from the back of the house and cut right across the yard to the driveway. As we got closer to the house we realized it was one of those two-story prefab jobs that look as if they just fall out of the sky and people move right into them. It didn't seem like anyone was living there, because the curtains were closed in all the windows.

At the end of the driveway we found the nervous, skinny Sandusky boy busy hammering away at a piece of metal with a large black rubber mallet. He had his back turned to us.

"Hello," Mac called.

But he kept on whacking.

"Sandusky!" I yelled louder.

There was still no response so I went up to him and tapped him on the shoulder. Big mistake. Sandusky spun around with the mallet and raised it above his head. His thyroid-disorder eyes opened so wide I thought his eyeballs would come tumbling out onto my face.

I shrieked as I ducked and tried to cover my face to stop the blow, but he froze with the mallet in midair. He relaxed his grip, took a set of tiny earphones out of his ears, and put the mallet down on the worktable behind him. He shook his head. "You scared me!"

"I scared *you*!" I barely managed to say, lifting myself out of my defensive crouch.

"Sorry," Sandusky said, as he wiped the sweat from his brow on the sleeve of his grimy, paint-smudged T-shirt. "We don't get many visitors around here."

"No wonder," Mac said. I could see she was taking a really good look at his face. Sandusky smiled at her, and it made him look less equine.

"I saw you guys at the hospital today, right? Hanging out with the body."

"We weren't hanging out with the body." Mac smiled back at him. I watched her surreptitiously loosen her ponytail and use her fingers to comb her hair forward. She always does that when she's getting ready to charm somebody.

"I don't know what you guys were thinking, but you should really think of taking up a hobby or something else," Sandusky said. "What are you doing here? You think you're some kind of detectives?" He let another smile loose on Mac. "Your mom's a coroner? That's what they said."

"We've helped the police to solve a few cases," I cut in so Mac didn't have to answer. I nodded to the worktable. "Is this your hobby: socking things with a mallet?"

"Actually, this is my rent," he said, circling and automatically lining up his tools like the husband in *Sleeping with the Enemy*. "Me and my grandpa get to live here pretty cheap in exchange for keeping up the place for the landlord. At the moment I'm trying to straighten out the aluminum siding." He pointed to the side of the house near the driveway where the siding was as warped as a fun-house mirror.

"And painting the fence," I said, holding out my paint-covered hand.

"You should wash that off with turpentine. There's some over there by the sink." Sandusky pointed to a corner of the garage.

As I headed for the sink, I overheard him talking to Mac in a slimy voice. I didn't like it one bit. If he was a nervous wreck at the murder scene, he didn't seem like it when he was chatting one-on-one with Mackenzie. He sounded slick, asking her about what she was studying and what year she was in at school.

I cleaned my hands fast, and scooted back to Mac's side. I finished wiping most of the paint off with a rag.

"So how long have you lived here?" I asked him.

"A couple of years," Sandusky said.

"You go to the Bronx High School of Science?" Mac asked, dropping her head to one side so her hair spilled and practically covered her face. "That was what Dr. Sagan said." She brushed her hair away using another of her techniques, which she had learned from the Bard: "A thing in motion would sooner catch the eye."

"Hey look, I don't mind the questions," he said, giving Mac another horsey grin. "But I gotta work." He

68

picked up the mallet and struck the strip of aluminum with a clang. "Yeah, I'm in my last year at Bronx Science."

Mac asked, "You said you live here with your grandfather, but where are your parents?"

"They moved to Atlanta last year. There was no way I was going to transfer in my senior year. I'm going to be a doctor like my grandpa was, and even my parents agree Bronx Sci is the best place to get on track for an Ivy and a med school."

"Med school?" Mac said, sounding too impressed for me.

"You bet," he said, giving the siding another smack. "I'm going to be an anesthesiologist."

"You're going to gas people?" I asked.

"No way," Sandusky said. "I'm not going to actually put people under. Well, maybe I'll do that for the first couple years, but then I'm going to work exclusively in the courts. I have an uncle who will hook me up. He gets paid anywhere from four to ten thousand dollars a day to show up for a malpractice trial as an expert witness. It doesn't matter which side hires him, he just tells them what they want to hear in medical terms and collects beaucoup bucks."

I knew even Mackenzie had realized he was beginning to sound like a real snot and conniver, because she was starting to pull her hair back into a ponytail. And when Mac wants to, her face can make her thoughts as clear as a bell. Right now she looked a touch nauseated, and grumbled, "You got it all figured out then."

"Yup." He grinned as he whacked the metal again.

"How long have you been working at the zoo hospital?" I asked.

"About eight months or so," he said. "Bronx Sci makes you do a mess of credits of community service so you don't graduate as a complete test tube. Besides, it's nearby, it gets me out of school early, and it's going to look like gold on my transcripts and college applications. Nobody's going to know it's such a pathetic little dump with dopes working there—I mean, the hospital part."

*WHACK.* He socked the siding again.

"God, you're smart," Mac said. I could tell she wanted to grab the mallet away from him and conk him on the nose with it.

"Yeah," Sandusky said, practically neighing. "Everybody's got the usual stuff on the transcript—helping the elderly and playing games with ghetto kids. What they don't know is that most of the suits reading those college admissions transcripts are chicks. And chicks go lovey-dovey with animals. And when a Harvard admissions chick gets my application and sees the letters Z-O-O, she's going to go lovey-dovey about me, and I'll be in like Flynn. Fingers crossed, of course."

Mac and I looked at each other. This was one sick puppy.

I decided to cut to the chase. "What we want to know is, what do you know about what happened to Ivan Allen?"

Sandusky stopped hammering, and saw we were glaring at him. All his flirting and bravura and know-it-all front faded in a flash. "You mean about his unfortunate passing?" he said, clearly picking his words very carefully now.

"Yeah," Mac said. "His *murder*."

"Oh," Sandusky said. He started to put his tools away in the garage, but we stayed close to him. He was beginning to look more like the nervous skinny horse-face we'd seen him as at the hospital. "Ivan may have transformed the zoo in the last few years, but . . ." We could see him working hard to say something. "Let's just say he was not the nicest person."

"How do you mean?" Mac quizzed.

"I didn't have to deal much personally with him. Most of what I know is from other employees—the people who worked with him. He was a control freak, they say. He made certain he was the lead name in every press release from the zoo. That's the kind of thing I've heard—you know, from Maxine."

"She told you a lot about him?" I asked.

"Her and Doc," he said. "Dr. Jahangir. I heard a lot from others—lots of the vets and zoologists—all kinds of workers. They talk at the staff cafeteria. Loads of people hated him. Dr. Sagan was the only one who ever said anything nice about him, and that always had something to do with fund-raising or one of his talk-show stints. Lots of people said Ivan had . . . personality shifts."

"Like what?" I asked.

"I heard that it happened when it was coming close to one of his media fiestas—like the *Tonight Show*. When there was an appearance like that, he would spaz out. Animal trainers who had to deal with him said he would lose touch with reality. Growl at people. I saw it once when there was a press conference about a new snow leopard. I was asked to help serve the snacks. And just before he was supposed to go up to the microphone, he grabbed me and shoved a cup of boiling hot coffee in my hand. 'This has whole milk!' he started to scream at me. 'I specifically asked for half-and-half!' So I said, 'But I didn't give you this.' 'Just do it!' he screamed at me like he was going to either rip my head off or keel over from a stroke."

"A lot of people saw that side of him?" Mac asked.

"Everyone has a story like that, usually much worse. People called Ivan 'Dr. Jekyll' behind his back. He was mentally ill, no question about it. Really sick."

Sandusky got a strange look in his eye, as if he'd said too much. When it was clear he was clamming up, Mac tried to loosen him up again by helping him move the rest of his tools and gear inside the garage. I turned my attention toward the house.

There was a worn lawn chair, the cheap kind you can adjust so it goes all the way back and your feet go up. I couldn't help but notice a couple of empty iced-tea glasses with squeezed lemon wedges sitting in the bottom of them. A newspaper lay on a wrought-iron table next to the chair. I picked it up automatically, and was surprised to see that it was in German.

"Hey," I called to Sandusky. "Who's reading the *Berliner Zeitung*? My German teacher brings it in to our class once in a while. . . ."

Sandusky looked stunned as he spun to face me. It was as though he had gone full circle and had been completely transformed back into the petrified wreck he'd been when we'd seen the cops questioning him.

He cleared his throat, looked at his watch, and said, "Sorry, I gotta go. I have a piano lesson."

We waited until he started to trot, and then we headed in the opposite direction.

"Bye," Mac called to him, pretending nothing was wrong.

"Yeah," Sandusky grunted without even turning around. Mackenzie and I walked until we saw Sandusky break into a lope and disappear around the corner. I grabbed Mac and started dragging her back to 573.

I could feel an uncontrollable yen for M&Ms and my palms getting clammy as, well, clams. "There's something wrong," I said.

"With what?"

73

"That German newspaper. It had their address on it and 'H. Sandusky' on the mailing label. That's got to be his grandfather, who not only reads it, but *subscribes* to it."

"So what?" Mac asked.

"I don't know," I admitted.

Mac looked confused. "That kid seemed to me to be a mad, mustachioed, purple-hued maltworm, anyway." I was glad to see my Shakespearean-quote T-shirts were having an effect on her.

We made it back to the freshly painted gate, which I carefully pried open with a stick.

"Are you sure we should be doing this?" Mac said, as we walked up to the front entrance of the house.

"Nope."

"I figured."

We peered through the small smudged windows that framed the front door. The way the afternoon sunlight struck them, we couldn't see anything much inside. Next we tried a couple of regular windows on the right side of the house. They had curtains *and* shades, so again we saw absolutely nothing. We walked around the other side of the house. There were thinner curtains on what looked like the kitchen windows.

"I think I saw a shadow moving," I whispered. It seemed to have moved off to the right into another room. I signaled Mac to follow me to the back of the joint. We stopped at another window, and this time we just stood there listening. Mac kept looking around, as if she expected Sandusky to pop up behind us swinging a chain saw.

I closed my eyes and strained to hear. It sounded like the floorboards or substandard Congolium tiles were creaking inside, and maybe a radio or TV was playing. I pulled Mac down so that we were crouched beneath the window. I told her as softly as humanly possible, "Do one of your cat sounds."

She does them better than anybody.

Mac looked at me as if I were deranged.

"Just do it!"

She shook her head, mouthing, "no way."

I furrowed my brow and scowled at her until she finally nodded her head.

"*Meeoow.*"

I signaled at her to do it again, as I scratched gently on the window with my fingernails.

"Meeeoooooow."

Mac looked really ticked off now, but I was busy scratching. I pointed at her like a conductor demanding another, still louder meow. Suddenly, she opened her mouth and let out a scream.

I followed her terror-filled eyes up to the window. The curtain was pulled aside, and there was a face. At first it looked like a cheap, translucent mask from a Halloween shop—but then the eyes in it blinked. The face, or what was left of it, was real—a parcel of rippled scar tissue that seemed almost reptilian. The variety of colors of the skin ranged from cadaver-white to dark, dark purple. The nose was almost not even there—a pair of air holes. The head was bald, but it was the eyes that really scared me. They looked right into mine like a greeting from the grave. What was most horrifying was that I could see there was a real intelligence behind the eyes—but with it, also, an appalling glaze of utter ferocity.

I screamed bloody murder, grabbed Mac's hand, and we ran for our lives. We booked it as fast as we could down the driveway, out the gate, and raced through the streets. We were all the way back to the zoo before I noticed my hand was again covered in white paint.

## 8

### Never Miss a Good Chance to Shut Up

**"What was that? What *was* it?"** Mackenzie gasped as I detoured us into one of the zoo's vehicle-repair garages right behind Astor Court. A mechanic wearing gray overalls with the name *Chip* embroidered in script on the front got me a tin can with some solvent in it and a sponge to get the paint off my digits once more. He looked at us as if he knew something was cockeyed—but he was polite enough not to be a Sherlock yenta about it. I waited until Mac and I were heading around the sea-lion tank before I even ventured a guess to answer her question about what we'd seen.

"That had to have been Pete's grandfather in the window," I said. "Or maybe he's some kind of scientist and a retort of nitric acid or liquid hydrogen blew up in his face. Whatever, he looks like he was involved in some kind of experiment that went *very* wrong."

Mac was trembling—either that, or my eyeballs were still twitching from the sight of the phantom in the window. "Like cloning trolls or ghouls," she said.

"It could be genetic research," I said. "They're doing

horrible things now like putting chicken heads on weasels and all kinds of other things."

"Well, there's something unspeakable going on in that house, let me tell you." Mackenzie yanked her hair back tighter against her scalp, ready for fight or flight. "Whatever it is, Peter Sandusky was trying to hide it from us. He thinks we're stupid."

"I never saw a nervous wreck who thought he was such hot stuff," I said. "At least Westside always beats Bronx Sci at lacrosse."

"Right!" Mac said.

I could see her turning her fright into anger, which is what she usually does when something really freaks her out. Lots of people try to make us give up whenever we're investigating any case, and for all kinds of reasons. Just because the old Sandusky looked like an albino mutant bogeyman didn't mean it had anything to do with the case, however.

"Lying Pete switched the blood," she said. "I just know it. He killed Ivan Allen."

"Hey," I said. "Pete may be planning to be an anesthesiologist, but I don't think he's been taking any Regents courses in sedating six-hundred-pound gorillas. Nobody I spoke to saw any teen weirdos or anyone else who looked out of place down at the Congo or backstage in the gorilla lab—and vice versa: zero *personas* could make it into the blood room at the hospital unless they belonged there, probably in whites, or they'd have stood out like a two-headed kangaroo at a Reverend Moon mass wedding."

"Well, somebody *did* drug a gorilla and take his blood and someone *did* monkey around in the blood room," Mac said.

I led the way into the administration building. Lieutenant Jamieson was still stationed at the threshold of the hospital annex and busy with his Bronx crew, but he gave us a nod. Zoode came over to deal with us. He seemed to be making a conscious effort to keep his puffy belly sucked in as he walked. "We're not finished in there," the sergeant said.

"Where's Perry?" I asked.

"He had to get something to eat," the Sergeant said. "Don't you two think you should go home? You know, whoever zapped Ivan Allen could still be around here."

"Yeah," Mac said. "Or in the neighborhood."

"You ought to check out the Sandusky family tree and see what's swinging up in its branches," I said. "It's worth a gander. But we've got other work to do around here."

"Like what?" Zoode asked.

"We really need access to Ivan's office," I told him. "There's got to be stuff in there you're going to need as soon as possible. By the time your experts get around to the hard drives, whoever killed Ivan Allen could be in Honolulu or Santiago."

Zoode mulled that over a moment. I could see the second his brain cells decided he had nothing to lose, and that he might get some free work out of us.

"Well," he finally said, "I've never seen a case shape up like this one. . . ."

"What do you mean?" I asked.

"Practically everyone around this place tells me they hated the victim and none of them have any alibis," Zoode said. "*And they don't seem to care.*"

He pointed us in the direction of the main hallway, and Mac and I took off. Ivan's office was midway down a long row of underprivileged-looking chambers, between Perry's and a conference room. One of those cheap black-with-white signs with Ivan's name on it was affixed to an open door. Inside, a couple of cop technicians I recognized from the blood room were finishing up dusting and snooping through his desk. A pair of old computers were sitting against the back wall.

"Sergeant Zoode said we can check the computers," I said. "Dr. Sagan knows about it, too."

"We're finished," one of the technicians grunted. They pushed by us and Mac and I marched straight to one of the practically antique Macintosh Performa 636CDs that stood on green, metal rolling tables. I pressed the ON button at the top-right of the keyboard, and turned on the monitor.

It took a minute before the screen came up and I was able to get on the Web. "We need to know more about

Ivan," I said, punching in his name. "A *lot* more." His own Web site popped up with a lot of baloney and stock publicity photos with him holding baby animals and flashing his phony smile on talk shows. We got out of there fast and pulled up the first ten of 319,785 references to Ivan Allen.

Mac checked her notepad and rolled her swivel chair up to the second computer. She got that one up to speed and typed in "Ivan Allen + Zoo." That narrowed the references down to articles about Ivan at the time he had his first big zoological assignment to the San Diego Zoo around a decade ago. You could see he had a press machine starting to work for him. He stayed at San Diego for five years and then did a couple of years at the St. Louis Zoo.

We had gotten the references down to under a thousand, but that was still too many. "It's more of his talk-show junk," Mac said, "and him getting the plum primate spot here at the Bronx Zoo six years ago. Most of the articles are all about him and his Congo and Gorilla Forest."

"This is all press-kit stuff," I moaned. "It still doesn't tell us anything personal. I think we have to go back further."

Mac flipped another page in her notebook. "Perry said he had cousins in Germany," she said.

"The *Berliner Zeitung*!" I blurted out, remembering the newspaper I'd seen at the Sandusky's. I tapped in "Ivan Allen + Germany."

There were 415 sites for that combo. Stuff like: Christopher S. Allen, "Transformation of the German Political Party System"; Milton J. Allen, "Charge and Field Effects in Biosystems"; and lots of referrals to German newspapers and magazines. I've had two years of German at Westside, and I could make out enough about sites like "Nacht der Kavaliere: Allen; Deutsche Gedichte" to know they weren't about Ivan Allen.

"Pay dirt," Mac said, staring at her screen.

I zipped my chair closer to hers and stared at her monitor. Mackenzie studies French and Latin, but she could recognize enough of the German to know the site on the screen might be important. "Here's Ivan, a zoo, and something about Stuttgart."

I clicked to bring up the original newspaper article for the reference. "It's about a fire," I translated. I'm not a brain in German, but I was doing the best I could. "It's about Ivan—and a fire at a zoo—the Stuttgart Zoo." I scanned the article, and learned that Ivan Allen had been the head of primate research there. The date on the article was fifteen years before. "A fire in his primate facility."

"What happened?"

"It says animals burned . . . baby chimps, gorillas—mandrills killed. Workers were injured . . . burned . . . a zoologist . . . a couple of lab workers . . . the whole primate building burned. . . ."

"This is terrible," Mac said.

I knew she was beginning to think along the same lines as I was, but the article was like a dam breaking. We couldn't even think of everything it meant, all the possibilities. Obviously it all had something to do with why Ivan Allen was killed—but I couldn't sort it all out in two seconds.

Mac was typing data in right and left on her computer. "I've got a related article on it in French." Her French is better than my German, which was a real plus. Within the next few minutes we had found three other articles and had them printing out.

"The names!" Mac was yelling. "Check the names of who was killed. Maimed. Anything."

I scrolled through everything I'd pulled up in German. There were a dozen or so names that meant nothing to me—except for Henning. "Henning," I said.

"As in John Henning, the flying groundskeeper in the bucket?" Mac said.

"Right. But this is Wilma Henning—she was in charge of . . ." I hesitated at several of the long scientific German words. They often tack them all together. "She had talking chimps. She was teaching chimpanzees how to talk." I kept refining the meaning. "Yeah, she was the teacher for a few chimps . . . highly trained . . . they could sign . . . speak . . . sign-speak . . . a couple of hundred words."

A thought struck me and I froze. Mac picked up on it right away. "What now?"

She peered at my screen as I typed in "Stuttgart + Paterfamilias."

A single reference popped up, one for an article in a German magazine. I clicked to bring up the original. It seemed to take forever before the article with photos was up on the screen. There was a face staring at us. A large hairy, dumbfounded face, with outraged eyes and an open mouth filled with large, frightening teeth. The caption to the photo read, "The prize lowland gorilla, Paterfamilias, burned to death along with his family in a fire at the Stuttgart Zoo."

"Oh, my God," Mackenzie said.

I looked at the proud silverback. I could imagine his family. His wife and the aunts. His baby gorilla kids.

"It means 'father of the family,'" Mac said. "Paterfamilias. That's what his name means, doesn't it—something like that?"

For the moment, I couldn't even speak.

## 9

### Labyrinth

**"Uh-oh," I finally said, just noticing** a red light the size of a period blinking at the top right corner of my screen, between the pen logo for WordPerfect and the date.

"What?" Mackenzie said.

"We're being spied on," I said, jumping up. I pointed to the flashing red dot. "Somebody's at another station—here at the zoo—someone's watching a screen and seeing everything we've brought up and printed."

Mac zipped her mouse upward to shut off her computer, but I stopped her in time. "No." I looked on the rulers and button bars to see if there was a code to tell who was monitoring, but there was nothing. No external gizmo near the hookups or on the floor. Not a single signal splitter in the room.

"Come on," I said, heading for the door. I pointed toward the old Performas. "Leave them on."

Mackenzie scooped up our printouts from the master bin, and raced after me into the hall. There had to be a central console in Perry's office to keep track of who was coming in on the system. Nearly every big organization and corporation's got that now to make sure the machines are being used for business and not joke e-mail and electronic shopping.

I scooted past the glass-windowed wall which defined Perry's office. The door to his office was locked. "Give me plastic," I told Mac.

Mac dug through her fake-leopard bag and gave me her Amex. Our parents had given us credit cards for emergencies, but they make us check with them before using them, unless we're someplace really grotesque and it's life or death. I shoved one end of the card in the crack to the left of the doorknob. The door wasn't high security, so I was able to trigger the lock release on my first swipe downward. It was as easy as using a debit card at Shop-Rite.

I opened the door and we went in. The central monitoring box was sitting next to a blue-and-gray iMac. Only two of the location lights were on, with all the systems' stations indicated clearly on a list. One of the lights was Ivan's Performas; the other light showed that someone in the Congo facility had linked itself in on our party.

"Let's catch whoever it is," I said.

Mac and I rushed back out, slamming the door behind us. Zoode was in the foyer.

"Did you find anything?" Zoode asked.

"Maybe," I said, as we flew by him. We went out the

door and headed down the center route of the zoo grounds. Mac tried to check the printouts in her hands as we hurried past the elephant and rhino area. The World of Reptiles was on our left, with the Mouse House and Marmosets straight ahead. A bank of storm clouds were heading toward us and the sky was darkening fast. It was still pretty early but it felt practically like twilight.

"Why did Ivan get all those 'Remember Paterfamilias' notes all through the years?" Mackenzie said, puffing. "Who would send them, and why did they freak him out? Who *wanted* him to remember?"

I yanked out my cell phone and pressed the number code for Jesus, our computer expert.

"What?" Jesus said, answering. I could hear him chewing; they always had an early dinner at his house.

"We need ya," I said.

"Shoot."

"Got a paper and pencil?"

"Yep."

I practically yelled what we knew so far, and told him we needed help checking on everything he could find on any Blessmans, Panduskys, Waterses, Hennings— anyone presently working at the Bronx Zoo who may have been connected directly or indirectly to Ivan Allen and the Stuttgart Zoo. Anyone who had any reason to carry a fourteen-year-old grudge against Allen. A grudge strong enough to want to kill him.

Mac grabbed the phone. "Find out exactly what relationship Wilma Henning has to John Henning." She shoved the phone back to me.

"Call or e-mail the stuff to me," I said. "I can check it from the computers here."

Jesus said he'd jump right on it and call us back. By now Mackenzie and I were coming close to the entrance to the Congo.

"You think we'll catch whoever was scoping us?" Mac said, as she stuffed the printed sheets into her shoulder bag.

"Maybe," I said as we hurried through the huge wooden gates and into the maze of tunnels. It seemed most of the zoo employees had punched their time cards and left to go home to put their feet up on La-Z-Boys and warm up some corn niblets and Chef Boyardee ravioli. Mac was thinking hard about something. "Whatsamatta?' I asked. "I can smell your brain burning."

She sucked in a big chunk of air, and looked up toward the canopy. "I was just wondering, how come if humans are descended from apes, why do we still *have* apes?"

As we crossed into the Congo a strange quiet seemed to fall over the whole zoo. The jaguar area was dead silent. About a hundred feet in, Mac and I had to pass through a turnstile and a metal revolving door which only allowed you in, not out. The sun was low on the horizon, and we could feel the twilight coming, the time when the land belongs to the hunters and the weak should seek their shelter if they know what's good for them.

Deeper into the maze, a nervousness began to grip the darkening air. The growing uneasiness was in the trees above us—birds and monkeys suddenly beginning to squawk, fighting for their cooping spots on the branches. A gazelle burst from behind a cluster of buttresslike mangrove roots, its hooves shaking the ground with startling power.

A few of the path lights trickled on as we reached the nexus of the glass tunnels—tunnels that bore through the jungle and would eventually link up to the main building and Primate House.

We passed a few of the interactive exhibits. Mac pointed out the pit of snakes where you could press a button and a speaker let out sounds that aroused a gaggle of cobras. Here, the large tunnel we had picked branched off yet again into four smaller ones. We took the one on the far right which had the sign above that read, TO THE GORILLA FOREST. We weren't more than a couple of hundred feet down that passage when all the lights in the exhibits went out.

"Omigod," Mac said.

"They must turn off the lights so the animals will know it's almost night and time to go to sleep or devour, or whatever they're supposed to do." There was the sound of thunder, and the storm clouds had cut out enough of the sun to make it look like an eclipse. There was only a faint glow from the main building that cut through the jungle.

As we passed the next exhibit I could barely read the RIVER HOGS AND THE BUSH MEAT TRADE sign on a railing.

"I remember going to a zoo a long time ago and the tour guide told us that the river hog is actually the closest relative to the elephant," Mac said.

"That tour guide must have been one of those out-of-work actors that are so bored, they make up stuff to keep themselves awake. I thought elephants were closest to those big rodents from South America."

"Capybaras?"

"Yeah."

"Well, maybe he *did* say capybara. Whatever, it was something really weird."

One of the hogs bounded toward us and stopped at the glass. It raised its head in the air and let out a series of grunts. It was pretty loud even through the glass. We got the message and hurried on as best we could in the deepening shadows.

Suddenly, there was a *BOOM*, like something being slammed against metal. It was like someone had run straight into one of the corrugated metal doors I'd seen earlier that had been used to shut off parts of the tunnels. We froze and listened.

Quiet.

"What was that?" I asked Mac.

"It didn't sound good," Mac said. "Hello?" she called out into the curve of the tunnel ahead.

There was no response.

I stood there sniffing like a dog, straining every one of my senses. A moment later, there came more of the loud *BAM-BAM-BOOM*-ing. The left side of my face began to twitch, and I could see Mac didn't like standing there in the shadows with large things angrily slamming into walls. Not good.

The racket finally stopped. I took Mac's hand and we walked farther down the tunnel. At a bend there was enough light for me to see a giant spiderweb up in the corner of an exhibit. At the edge of the web was a black spider with a body the size of a champagne cork.

"Mac, you gotta check this out," I said to her.

"What?"

"Up *there*. In the corner."

I knew she saw it when she wrinkled her nose. I snuck my hand around her shoulder and brushed against the top of her ear with one of my fingers. She screamed, then spun like a whirling dervish until she could see the smile on my face.

"You're an immature idiot," she said.

My smile got even bigger.

"Did you hear that?" she asked.

"Of course I did."

She looked really ticked off. "Not me. Something *else*."

I listened.

And then I heard it. It sounded a little like an asthmatic wildcat and it made me uncomfortable. Whatever it was, you could tell it wasn't behind glass.

"There's something in this tunnel with us," Mac said. But then there was silence once more, and Mac and I pressed on to a point where the tunnel split yet again. One of the paths was blocked by a large metal gate.

"I guess we're going this way," I said as I led the way down the only open path.

We were barely into that tunnel before a strange odor filled the air. Mac lifted the collar of her shirt over her nose. "They spend millions for all this and then they get cheap with the Lysol," she said. She stopped still and was looking down at something on the floor. I looked down at it too. There was enough light spill here to see that it was a carrot—a half-gnawed piece of carrot the size of a crooked finger.

Mac picked up the carrot with the tips of her fingers, then let it drop. "It's wet," she said. "Covered with dribble." She was about to wipe her hands on her jeans, then opted to rub the dribble off on a slab of the glass.

We took a few steps more and heard an animal scream, somewhere in front of us. We looked but couldn't see anything in the darkness ahead.

But—

We could hear breathing.

It was quick, scared breathing—and it must have

sounded a lot like mine. My eyes strained in the darkness. I took a step forward, and Mac fell in behind me. Her hand grabbed mine, both damp with sweat.

Now came a low whining, a lot like my neighbor's Doberman, who sticks its nose by the crack of the door and mewls for hours when he's left alone. But whatever was in that corner of the blackness now was no dog or your run-of-the-mill vermin.

We had to know what it was, so we stepped forward. I could sense it was bigger than a bread box but smaller than a goat. It was then that I saw what looked like two diamonds in front of me. After a moment, I could tell they were eyes.

"How cute," Mac said. She can always see better in shadows and darkness than I can. Even when I could make out the shape of the baby gorilla with its pointed ears, I wasn't too happy to see it.

"The baby's name is Elf," I said.

Mac laughed. "I can see why."

I wanted to believe Elf was behind really clear glass, but when I reached out toward him, the baby shrieked. He covered his face with his hands and the nub end of another carrot fell out of his grasp and rolled on the floor toward us.

Mac stood transfixed. The baby gorilla suddenly started freaking out now, screaming and panting, and shaking his hands as if it were being electrocuted. Mac picked up the remnants of his carrot and held it out for him. Elf's little wet nostrils were trembling.

"I'm not sure you should do that," I said.

Mac ignored me as Elf reached out for her. The baby's fingers touched the carrot and grasped it. He brought the carrot to his mouth and started chewing on it. A moment later, Elf put the carrot down and held out his hands to Mackenzie, as if he wanted her to pick him up.

Then we heard a different sound.

Mac and I looked behind us. There was a rectangle of light, as if a door had been opened.

A moment later, and there came the sound again. It was a very deep grunt that this time swelled until it was transformed into a reverberating, deafening roar. The massive silhouette of Gargantua filled the end of the tunnel.

"It can't be," Mac said.

But it *was*. Elf's father paused and roared again. He began to pound his chest with the thunderous thump of a kettle drum, and there were neither bars nor glass between us and this bristling, lethal six hundred pounds of fury.

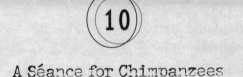

## 10

### A Séance for Chimpanzees

**Mac and I stood very still.**

The baby cried out again.

We watched as the form of Gargantua began to move toward us through the shadows. He was massive, powerful, outraged—approaching with a chilling deliberateness. I grabbed Mac and we slowly backed away, wanting to get out of the space between the silverback and his son. Elf saw his father but seemed much more interested in watching us retreat. Just as we were about to fade into the comfort of complete darkness, Gargantua roared and pounded his chest again.

Elf kept his eye on us, too—especially Mackenzie. He looked as though he still wanted to hang with us, but I motioned him to stop. "Just stay put," I whispered to the baby. "Stay. . . ."

The baby saw my hand signal, and looked at it quizzically. Then he cried out as if he wanted to play with us. A shard of reflected light let me glimpse the fear in Mac's eyes, and she must have seen much more of the same in mine.

Another roar from the end of the hall echoed like a sonic boom.

"Go to Daddy," Mac told Elf.

Elf cried even louder.

We turned and started to walk like those speed walkers I see all the time at the reservoir in Central Park who look really weirdissimo. And that's exactly how we looked, but I didn't care. Mac and I reached a bend in the tunnel and then broke into a sprint. We ended up smack at another locked, metal revolving door. There was no way out now.

"We gotta go back the way we came," Mackenzie said, as if announcing our death sentence.

We heard the patter of feet. Close. Very close.

"Just freeze," I said.

It was the baby looking for us—and we knew who'd be joining the party really soon. Mac and I instinctively backed ourselves against one side of the tunnel—our hands pressed against cold glass. The same thick glass meant to keep out predators was certainly going to keep Mac and me caged in.

We watched as the silhouette came around the bend of the tunnel. When I had first seen Gargantua in the habitat, when I was with Betty Waters, he had looked no bigger than a Volkswagen. Now he looked like a stretch Hummer. His head lowered menacingly.

Without moving my head, I wheezed to Mac. "Get on the floor and play dead."

We both carefully lowered ourselves onto the cold tile floor. I remember reading somewhere that that was what you were supposed to do when some big animal has you cornered, except for loner black bears, who rarely attack (but when they do, it's to enjoy you as a quivering mass of steak tartare).

As we lay on the floor, Elf raced over to Mackenzie and began to play with her hair.

"No, baby," Mac said. "No."

Gargantua roared ferociously at the sight. He was upright now, expanding and puffing himself up to his total enormity. Even Elf screamed with fright at the charge of his father, who halted in front of us. He raised his fists and began to pound on the tiles and glass and metal of the revolving door. He struck out at anything that could make a deafening noise.

I lay in a ball in front of Mac. We both had pulled our legs up close to our chests, and covered our heads and faces with our arms and hands. I peeked through my shaking fingers and saw the baby run straight through Gargantua's legs.

Gargantua grabbed hold of the sleeve of my shirt and pulled on it. He tossed me several feet across the floor, and then loped slobberingly to my side. I was rolled as tight as an armadillo now, and he shrieked, and banged the metal of the revolving door next to me until I thought my eardrums would rupture.

For a moment I thought he would leave, but he spun

and suddenly poked my side with his finger. He partially lifted me up and began to examine me. As he sniffed me a mist of his hot saliva painted my scalp. Somehow, both Mac and I managed to stay motionless, and for the first time in my life I really understood what the expression "scared stiff" is all about.

Gargantua let go of me and let out a series of grunts, culminating in a final roar and victory chest pounding. He turned and picked up Elf, who had crept back and was yanking at his leg hair. Elf was still chattering as they disappeared back around the bend of the tunnel.

When the squealing and pitter-patter of gorilla feet had long disappeared, Mac and I uncoiled. She shook her head, and smiled with relief at me. Me, I wasn't smiling. I was scared to death. This was my nightmare come true. Then I got angry. Really angry. Those gorillas hadn't gotten out into the tunnel by accident. Someone had let them in. And that someone thought they could try to kill us—or scare us off the case.

Well, I had news for them—they were dead wrong on both counts. With Mackenzie's help, I was personally going to nail them to the wall. After I finally got my breath back.

Mac and I got up off the ground. "Are you okay?' she asked. "Did that big ape break any of your bones?"

"No," I said. "How about you?"

She felt her arms and legs. "No damage," she said, as there came a ringing in her handbag. Mac fumbled through it and pulled out her crimson Audiovox. She flicked the phone open. It was her mom.

*What does she want?* I mimed to Mac as she struggled to sound normal. Mac made a grimace, urging me to find a way out of the tunnel. I moved my hands slowly over the wall behind us. Now when I pushed on the revolving door, the lock had been released. Mackenzie kept talking to Mrs. Riggs as I guided her into the main foyer of the primate building. When it looked like we were really safe from any more gorilla attacks, I cozied up to Mac so I could hear Kim too.

"No, nothing's wrong," Mackenzie told her mother.

"You sound like you're puffing," Mrs. Riggs said. "Your voice is funny. What's going on over there?"

Mac kept her eye on me to make certain she was saying the right thing. "We had trouble getting through a revolving door," she said. "It was stuck—but we're fine now. Mom, we think we're on to something. There's a lot going on. We think we really know the motivation—the reason Ivan Allen was killed. I mean, we have an idea—"

"I don't care," Mrs. Riggs said through the static on the phone. "I've thought about it, and I don't want you or P.C. staying at the zoo tonight. I already called Perry and told him. P.C.'s aunt called me, too—"

"But we're on the verge—" I blurted out, so she could hear me. "We're close to—"

Mrs. Riggs grunted to acknowledge me. She knew

Mac and I always practically glue our ears to the same phone. "P.C., I don't care what you two are on the 'verge' of. You can go back tomorrow in the daytime if you want, and I'm certain the same verge will be there. Mackenzie, your father and I are leaving for a poker game tonight near the uptown N.Y.U. campus. You know, those two philosophy professors and the one who teaches the film course and always makes your father talk about *Nosferatu* and *The Butcher's Wife*. We'll pick you and P.C. up on the way home—around ten-thirty."

"Make it eleven?" I insisted.

"We need the time," Mac added.

There was a pause. Dr. Riggs is really hard to put one over on. "You got it," she said, finally. "But no later. I spoke to Lieutenant Jamieson. He and his men are really confused on this one."

"I don't blame them," I said.

"What?" Mrs. Riggs said. The static began to shatter the call.

"Bye, Mom," Mac yelled. "You're breaking up."

Mackenzie flicked the phone shut. She looked behind her toward the revolving door, shivered, and started to follow me through the eerie red light of the lobby.

"It's got to be more than one killer, doesn't it?" Mac said.

"Or an eight-armed paperhanger."

"But how's it all connected to Stuttgart and the fire?"

"Ah, that's what we've got to find out," I said.

I jumped when I saw two scarlet specters suddenly coming toward us, but then I realized it was only a reflection of Mac and me in a mirrored partition. I stopped a second to straighten out my hair and pull my sweatshirt down from above my belly button. The gorilla had whacked me around worse than I thought— I looked like a real doofus. Mac used a Kleenex to help wipe the last of the gorilla slobber from my brow.

"Why do I feel like we're expected," I said, pushing open the pair of swinging, black metal doors marked STAFF ONLY. "Whoever sent Gargantua knew he more than likely wasn't going to kill us."

"Could've fooled me. What's next?" Mac said. "A pool of crocodiles?"

"We'll find out soon enough," I said.

We went by the holding booth Betty Waters had shown me. At least there were a few thirty-watt light-bulbs and skylights in the ceiling of the hall. A ghostly glow of the stormy sunset bounced through the far wall of jalousies behind the glass that framed the main habitat.

"That's where they sedate the gorillas for dental work and appendectomies, or whatever gorillas have," I said. There was the sound of more thunder—three or four strikes one after the other. Soon, because of the rain clouds and the thick canopy surrounding the building, any glimpse of outside looked like pitch black.

We followed the hallway signs to the primate nursery.

The whole Congo and pod seemed emptied of workers, and there was no sign of the cops or the forensic technicians hanging around any longer. As the hall curved we could see the glass door to Betty's domain. She was sitting in a swivel chair holding a tiny monkey and feeding it from a baby's bottle. There was a strange flickering light, and her head was down, so I guess we were supposed to think she didn't see us coming.

"Wait until you get a load of this," I told Mac, and opened the door.

When we entered, Betty looked up. She sat in the midst of a couple of dozen burning white taper candles, like a crystal-reader or fortune-teller. "The electric company's pulling one of its brownouts," she said. "Thank goodness all the chimpanzees love candlelight."

The suckling baby chimp in her arms was in a swaddling cloth, and she was rocking it like a human baby. It wasn't more than eight inches long, and for some reason the whole vision of this bizarre madonna and the burning candles made it seem as if Mac and I had walked in on a really scary Off-Broadway show. Along with Mackenzie and me in the audience, were a half-dozen big chimp females clutching their older, hairier babies. We all looked at Betty Waters as though she were the center tableau for a very low-budget Cirque du Soleil.

"This is my pal, Mackenzie Riggs," I told Betty.

"Yes," Betty said. "Perry told me you two would be

working together. It's very nice to meet you, Mackenzie. How are things going with you two?"

We didn't have any time to waste, and her phoniness was getting on my nerves. "*Gargantua didn't kill us*," I said, "if that's what you mean."

"Excuse me," Betty said, her inflated lips pursed as if in genuine puzzlement. "What are you saying?"

I was still shuddering from the adrenaline pulsing through me. "Only that Mackenzie and I were in your little maze out there, when someone made certain Gargantua was free enough to give us a special greeting."

"We could have been killed," Mac said.

Betty opened her eyes wide. "Gargantua got loose?"

"Yeah," I said.

"Omigod." Ms. Waters sounded about as excited as if she were listening to thirty hours of ice-skating music.

"You should have been there," Mac said, meaning it.

"All those gates and doors are on a master control console," Betty said. "Computers govern the animals. We're always very careful about all the doors and cages. One of the technicians must have made a terrible mistake." I had heard this patronizing tone from her before.

On the plus side, she wasn't wearing her wicker wig tonight. Her own hair was mud-brown and thin, with broken ends. I didn't know how to get around to all we had to grill her on. I noticed a computer and a monitoring indicator in a corner near a desk. "We know about Stuttgart and the fire," I said. "About all the dead animals."

"Yes," Betty said, her eyes locked on us like lasers now. "I know you do."

"And *we* know you do, too," Mac added.

## 11

### Smoke and Mirrors

**Betty petted the nursing monkey's tiny head** as it drank from the bottle in her hand. She dabbed at the mix of white formula and mother's milk that leaked from the trembling lips, and the monkey's eyes stared up gratefully.

"There, there . . ." Betty cooed.

She turned her chair toward a panel of levers. The first lever brought up a soft blue light on an atrium behind the row of primate incubators. In addition to chimp mothers and babies in the nursery, it appeared that there were a couple of Rhesus and baboon babies in with the ailing and premature bunch.

Betty moved another set of levers and a vast panorama of the indoor gorilla habitat could be seen about fifty feet away, like some sort of geodesic dome on a botanical garden or a lush adjoining dining room at Tavern on the Green. The rain fell on the ferns and lianas of the alley, and dribbled like tears down the windows. The members of the big contented gorilla family were all watching from behind the wall of glass. Elf was with Mama; nearby were Auntie "Hear No Evil," Uncle

Jimbo, and the other uncles and aunts. And Gargantua. Their gaze was riveted on the nursery and Betty with the cages of chimps—and the baby in her arms.

And us.

"You cannot work here without knowing how much like humans these animals are," Betty said. "They *are* people. They feel and think as we do. You can see it in their eyes. They love and have joy and feel pain just as we do. Do you know that we share 98 percent of the same genes with primates?"

I took a moment to try to figure out what Betty was up to, because the tone of her voice had changed, as if she were playing a cello solo for our benefit. I decided it was best to just charge forward. "Were you in Stuttgart for that fire at the zoo?"

"No."

"Were you ever there?" Mac asked.

"Never. I have never been in Germany," Betty said. "I've read about it—about the fire. I've been told about it. It was a terrible thing . . . so many animals killed . . . more frightfully than you can imagine. Important zoologists hurt. Workers burned."

"Sandusky's grandfather was there, wasn't he?" Mac said. "That's what happened to him . . . to his face?"

"Yes," Betty said. "The fire mutilated him physically, and its pain and horror drove him out of his mind."

"Are you saying he's crazy?" Mac asked.

Betty nodded as she wiped the baby's face gently and

placed its frail form back in the incubator. She slowly and carefully checked on the other, healthier-looking babies, giving them all a stroke on the head or a rub on the belly. "I was told the screams of the animals were an awful thing," she went on. "The gorillas—the babies—burning to death—being burned alive. There are those who were there who went insane. Workers who never regained their sanity, who were never the same again. Like poor Dr. Sandusky. He's wanted revenge for so long. . . ."

"He killed Ivan Allen?" I asked.

"Ivan Allen was a 'stranger fig,'" Betty said. "That is what Dr. Sandusky always called him. It is a special kind of fig that is found only in the Congo. Its seed is deposited by monkey dung up high in the mangroves, and it begins to grow among the fruit bats and owl-faced monkeys. The seed grows roots, sending them down to earth, and its vines grow and grow until it strangles and kills the whole tree. That is what Ivan Allen has always been like."

I caught Mackenzie's eye and gave her my I-don't-think-we-should-buy-everything-we're-hearing look.

"Did Sandusky send the 'Remember Paterfamilias' notes all these years?" Mac asked, sitting in a plastic scoop chair. She continued going through the printouts, looking for more details. I saw she had begun to scribble down names she was finding in the articles.

"Sandusky believed Ivan set the Stuttgart fire *deliberately*?" I asked Waters.

"Believed?" Betty said, as though insulted. "He knew!"

"Why?' I wanted to know. "Why would Ivan set fire to a part of his own zoo? Why are you laying all this on us and not the police?"

Ms. Waters had moved so that the incubators and the primate habitat became her background. "I don't know," she said. "Perhaps I am asking for understanding and mercy from you."

I think Mac and I both almost passed out when we heard that one.

"Ms. Waters, you must have figured the police would have found the connection to the Stuttgart fire eventually," Mac said.

"Not necessarily," Betty said. "I've spoken to them. They're looking for someone who hated Ivan for his stardom. Who wanted his place. Oh, I read in the paper how the detectives on a case sometimes check out a victim's visits to recent Web sites. A few computer things like that. But they don't search. Ivan was in the public eye. No one has ever dreamed of his guilt—his guilt for the fire so many years ago. They never prosecuted him for that."

"Why did Sandusky blame Ivan for a fire that was an accident?" Mac asked.

"It *wasn't*," Betty practically yelled at us. "Sandusky and other scientists, zoologists, knew there was talk of a very large insurance claim made by the Stuttgart zoo. It provided the funds Ivan needed to promote himself in more important quarters: London and the United States. The insurance funded his startling lion habitat in Germany, a showpiece he had planned, which gave him the credentials he needed to be noticed by the global zoo players."

"He planned the fires?" I said.

"Oh, yes. If you check back further in some of the smaller local German papers you find there were smaller fires a month, two months before the major conflagration. That is how Ivan set up the main fire. Little fires blamed on children. Delinquents."

"Just like the recent fires here?" Mac asked.

"Yes," Betty insisted. "Sandusky knew Ivan was getting ready to burn again. He would burn the primate facility. There would be the staggering payment by the insurance companies, funds to be used for his future pandas. Yes, Ivan would get his purchase from China one way or the other—and Sandusky already knew very well the way it would be. That is why Dr. Sandusky had to act. In his madness, he knew he could not allow the horror to happen again. He would kill the strangler root. Peter heard him saying that. Yes, he would pull the strangler root out and stop it once and for all.

"The doctor would prowl the grounds here at night, long after the zoo had closed. He would see Ivan working here, watch him through the vast windows of the Congo forest. He had been out there for years. Seven or eight years ago he had moved here. I caught him one night and he told me his secret about Ivan. Dr. Sandusky's not the monster he appears to be."

"The phantom of the zoo," Mac said.

"Yes. When the little fires started he knew he would have to move quickly. He must have put the sugar into Ivan's coffee. . . ."

There were two shadows moving along a translucent window to the hall. Mackenzie and I jumped, thinking only of Gargantua. The door opened and in came John Henning and Peter Sandusky. They looked to Betty. She shook her head.

"I imagine you're going to tell the police everything you know?" she asked us.

"We have to," I said.

"You don't have to," Betty said threateningly.

"Oh yes, we do," Mac said.

"Don't you two go to school?" Mr. Henning said, glaring at us. "You'd better go home, and don't come back to this zoo."

Mackenzie gathered her papers and stood up. I waited until we had made our way past the two guys before I opened my big mouth.

"I don't know," I said, as simply as I could. "We think there's a lot to learn around here."

I made certain I closed the door fast behind us, then grabbed Mackenzie's hand, pulling her along after me. There were sounds like electric doors and locks being switched on and off.

"Here's a list of everyone I could find mentioned in the Stuttgart fire," Mac said, "the workers, zoologists—anyone who was listed as injured or working there at the time. There are probably others, and, of course, they all had parents and relatives. A lot of people were affected by it."

I glanced over the names to see if anything would pop out at me besides Wilma Henning. The list wasn't long, but it was more international than I expected: Anna Preziosi, Maurice Benet, Adolph Kleinberg, Friedrich Hofmansthal, Hidegarde Kipphardt, Dr. Herman Sandusky, Elise Wasser, Anton Jodermann, Johann Ulbricht . . . and a half dozen other names. The Stuttgart Zoo was bigger than I thought.

"I only recognize Henning and Sandusky," Mac said.

"Yeah," I said. "But maybe we're missing something."

"Like what?"

"I don't know."

Now there was the noise of what sounded like a garage door slamming down very hard somewhere just ahead. We got past the primate holding tank and back out into the main lobby, but the revolving door we'd entered through was locked. We tried every door and doorway working clockwise around the lobby. It became clear there was only one passageway left open for us, and we raced down it.

Several other doors and passageways were closed, but each time, we'd find the one that let us move along.

Finally, one of the doors led outside and, since it was night, we figured we didn't even have to worry about animals.

The sky had opened up and the rain was coming down with a ferocity I had not known since I first moved to New York City. The rain fell in slanting sheets, whipped by gale-force winds.

As we made our way past the back side of the Congo land, the stinging rain smacked against our faces and eyes. Other than the sound of the rain, the zoo had fallen completely quiet. I remember thinking, Now the animals can feel that they are back in the wild with the torrential winds and angry rain.

Mac and I knew we'd have to circle all the way around to find our way back past the World of Darkness. We got to one gate, but the way was dark, and there was nothing I could recognize.

I checked out what looked like a darkened ticket booth beside the gate. I tried the door handle every which way, but that sucker was locked tight. Farther up the path we finally saw a couple of lights on in what looked like a bunker. When we got to the door there was a blue sign that said RESTRICTED AREA. I knew it was a waste of time because there was no way it would be open. But I reached down anyway and turned the handle—and it turned. Then I tried pushing the door open—and it opened.

We burst inside laughing and dripping rain all over

the place. My eye immediately looked for the gorillas. There were none.

A flash of headlights splashed against the wall inside the room. I opened the door and watched the headlights getting closer until I saw that they belonged to one of those little electric golf carts. And the cart kept stopping and the guy in it would look around. I thought it had to be a security guard, so I ran out into the rain. I waved and waved until the golf cart driver saw me.

The cart parked in front of the building and the guy got out wearing a huge green rain poncho with the hood over his head. I motioned for him to come inside. He grabbed a duffel bag off the cart and followed me in.

"Thanks for stopping," I said. "It's really coming down out there!"

The guy took a look around the inside of the room, and put the duffel bag on the table. As Mac was trying to dry her hair with a roll of paper towels she said, "Yes, thanks a lot."

He turned to face us. Placing his hands on his hood, he pulled it back. At first I thought the man was wearing a wet white scarf, but then I realized it was his own skin.

Mac dropped the roll of paper towels onto the floor.

We had seen that face once before, but this time we were beyond screaming.

## Stalking

**I no longer felt the wet clothes on my back** nor my feet swishing around in my shoes as I backed up. In fact, a rabid triceratops could have been passing three feet behind me and I wouldn't have noticed.

All I could be certain of was the disfigured human form standing before Mac and me. And it wasn't so much Dr. Sandusky's scars and mutilation that startled me now. I mean, you see everything on the streets of New York. It was his eyes—the doctor's swollen and savage brown eyes utterly set and determined to do evil.

"You . . . were asked to . . . leave," the voice wheezed through the two glistening, thin chalky strips that were his lips, "and yet here you are." He slid his duffel bag along the table toward us as we backed ourselves up against the wall beside the TV monitors.

He focused on Mackenzie. I saw her shudder, and immediately her hand grabbed hold of mine.

"Didn't John . . . make it clear to you?" he whispered through clenched, twisted teeth. "John . . ."

"Mr. Henning?" I said. "We . . ." I tried to get my

voice to make audible sounds. "We didn't mean . . . to disturb you . . ." I said. I so wanted Mac and me to just get out of there—out of the building and away from this very deranged, very angry man. "Mackenzie's mother is coming for us," I said, absurdly.

"Yes, we have to be going," Mac told him.

"We won't say anything."

He looked with utter madness right into my eyes.

"I don't believe you," he said. He zipped open his blue canvas bag on the table and reached into it. When his hand came out it was holding the handle of what seemed to be a long, thin paddle in a beat-up brown leather case. He unbuttoned the end of the case with his thumb, and as he pulled the instrument out, you could hear the scraping of a blade against a sharpener that had been sewn into its sheath.

It was a machete like the ones I've seen Africans using in movies about hunting tigers or clearing jungle to lay train tracks. But not just some regular Watusi or Guatemalan machete; this one looked like a model designed by NASA. The blade looked like titanium and shimmered in the white halogen lights on the ceiling. Dr. Sandusky held the machete like it was an extension of himself, pointing it at me and rolling it over to check its cutting edge.

"This cleared my way through ten miles a day of the thickest jungles of the Amazon. It'll cut through the trunk of a rubber tree in one slice." A smile formed on his lipless slit of a mouth, and it stretched what was left of his skin so tightly across his face we could see the outlines of his teeth beneath it.

He narrowed his eyes like a cougar about to leap. There was nowhere to run. When I saw his hand clench the machete as hard as he could, I knew our only chance would be for Mac to get out of there alive and get help. As he raised the blade, I suddenly pushed Mac clear to his left. Sandusky's eyes followed her like a bull distracted by a fluttering red cape, but he had committed to bringing his machete down as hard as he could straight at me. I ducked as the blade cut through the air and sliced right into the wall three inches from my ear.

"Run!" I yelled at Mac. "Run! Get out of here!"

Dr. Sandusky tugged his blade free from the wall and raised the machete again. Mac ran, but before she did I saw the terror in her eyes—the fear that her best friend was about to become sushi. She screamed, and again Sandusky lowered the blade with the speed of a falling guillotine. This time I darted left and wound up behind a wall of monitors.

Within a second the machete was slicing diagonally through the air right toward me. I saw the doctor's tongue edge hideously out of his mouth as I tried to duck. The blade swooshed just above my head and carved right into the side of a TV and its wires, sending out a shower of sparks and glass.

He blinked, and I ran for it.

I heard the madman's grunts and wheezings as he swung again. I don't know how close he came. I was out the door following Mac, and now she and I were both running down a hallway and deep into what began to look like the Congo and Gorilla Forest's main animal-treatment area. I caught up to her as we ran past a couple of operating tables and chairs with clamps to restrain large primates. It looked like a torture chamber. I knew it was one place I didn't want Dr. Sandusky to catch us.

We kept running, through another doorway and down yet another hallway. As we turned right I prayed for it not to be a dead end. We didn't have a clue where we were going. All we knew was that a homicidal maniac in a poncho was chasing us with a machete.

Sandusky began to close in on us, so I grabbed the nearest thing—a rolling cart with Erlenmeyer flasks and bottles of distilled water on it. I pushed it in his direction, but I never saw Sandusky run into it. All I heard was a crash, and the sound of the doctor growling like an animal. When I glanced back, I could see he was on his feet again, his head bleeding.

I sprinted, catching up to Mac just as she skid to a halt at a red box on the wall. She smashed the glass with her house keys, and pushed the button inside the box. An alarm blasted. "That alarm may save lives, but it's going to make us deaf," I heard Mac yell.

We ran around another bend. Ahead of us was a

single door, and on the door was a picture of a big spotted cat and a sign that read EXTERIOR JAGUAR PADDOCK. QUALIFIED PERSONNEL ONLY.

Dr. Sandusky came into sight around the bend. He was walking swiftly, confident that we were trapped.

"It's night," I whispered excitedly to Mac. "The jaguars are all locked up inside."

"We don't know what their bedtime is," she said. She glanced back to see the wheezing doctor approaching, clutching his machete. Mac pushed the door open.

And out we went.

The door closed behind us. And now we were out in lush jungle, but there was something different. Very different. The rain had stopped, and a night mist was rising from the ground to form a thick knee-high layer of fog that covered the bases of rocks and grass and mangrove roots.

We were moving quickly forward when the door behind us was flung open. The silhouette of Dr. Sandusky with his blade raised filled the doorway. He saw us and charged forward. I grabbed Mac's hand and we darted left and right through the maze of trees. A gust of wind kicked up tongues of the fog and rolled over Sandusky. There were the sounds of him tripping, and we picked up speed until we couldn't even see him any longer.

Exhausted, Mac and I had to stop to catch our breath. We listened.

No sounds.

No Sandusky.

No jaguars.

"Please let sleeping cats lie," I mumbled. Near the perimeter, a few lights from the outer zoo walk let us see that the sides of the enclosure at this point had high concrete walls—way too high to climb up. The farthest barrier was a moat and a thirty-foot-high chain-link fence.

That was our only chance.

"What if there are alligators in the moat?" Mac asked.

"No way," I said. "The Congo only has crocs." I thought I was kidding, but I realized anything was possible. Between us and the closest edge of the moat seemed to be about a hundred yards, with dense thickets of mangroves on the left and right. The alarm was still screaming, and it sounded like the rest of the zoo animals were freaking out about it. I heard elephants trumpeting, lions rumbling like giants, and the monkeys in the trees shrieking crazily.

The fog kicked up as we got closer to the moat, where the ground dipped sharply. Mac tripped on one of the roots, so I grabbed her arm and we tried keeping each other up. I didn't want to tell Mac I was remembering all the documentaries I'd see of large cats like jags and cheetahs that excel at climbing trees. I knew how often they'd kill their prey and then drag it up into a tree, wedge it between a couple of branches, and dine at leisure.

I heard a creaking in the branches and my head

whipped up. I figured it was my imagination, but my eyes scanned the shadows of the trees for any outline of a large cat.

Nothing.

When we were within fifty yards of the moat, Mac and I heard a sound that made us stand dead still. It was the unmistakable growl of a cat.

We had only thirty yards to go before the fence.

"We're gonna have to run for it," I whispered to Mac.

She nodded her head, and we bolted through the gauntlet of trees. We heard something behind us. Something large. But we didn't look back. We kept pumping our legs as hard as we could. Just as we were about to come out from the mangrove trees and into the clearing I saw something rise out of the mist right in front of us.

It was large.

Just a few feet away.

It was Dr. Sandusky.

We were about to run into him, or I should say, run into his slicing machete. Mac and I stopped short, but our feet hit a slick and slid out from under us. I felt the breeze from the blade as it cut through the air and ground fog just in front of my face. Sandusky was right above us, and we struggled to edge ourselves backward through the mud and the mist. There was no time to get up. No time to breathe or to defend ourselves—or to do anything but die.

Sandusky raised the machete one last time above his head and as he did, I thought, This is it, for Mac and me. We fought the good fight. And this is how it ends. Then I heard something. Sandusky heard it too, and froze. It was the type of sound that makes you stop what you're doing.

Something sprang out of the mist on the other side of Sandusky. It tackled him, bringing him to the ground, and he screamed. A massive jaguar was on top of him, yanking him around. His body twisted and shook.

Mac and I were up from the ground—but now there were four other cats around us, their heads rising out of the ground fog. A couple of them were smaller, maybe a hundred or so pounds, but there were two larger ones, each weighing maybe two hundred and fifty pounds. The jags stepped closer, their bodies hugging the ground.

They were closing on us. The largest had hunkered down low, crouched. His eyes focused right at us as he snarled and displayed a mouthful of night-black gums and large, yellow teeth.

That was when we heard the strange sound above us, and I looked up. It was the bucket from the crane lowering down toward us with John Henning at its controls! The jaguars ran off, disappearing into the forest of vines and mangrove trees.

Henning grabbed Mac and me and pulled us into the bucket with him. As the gondola cleared the fence we could still see the spot where Sandusky's body had lain. There were left only the tattered remains of a green-and-yellow poncho and the silvery glint of his machete. Somewhere up in the screaming branches of the mangroves—later—someone was going to have go bring down whatever pieces were left of Dr. Sandusky.

## 13

### Hardening Evidence

**So much more had happened** by the time Mac's mom and dad arrived at the Fordham Road Gate from their poker game. Perry and Lieutenant Jamieson waited with us at the entrance to the administration building, while one of the zoo's custodians met them with a couple of jumbo black umbrellas. We watched Kim and Dr. Riggs park their old Volvo, get out, and slosh their way around the still-spewing gilded swan fountain. The rain was coming down like bullets and the sky was continuing to grumble and light up with thunder and eerie blue lightning.

They resembled a funeral cortège as they came up the sweep of brick steps from the courtyard and barged into the lobby. Perry Sagan leaped forward, a mellifluent and distinguished-looking jack-in-the-box. He was off and running with hugs and small talk for Mac's parents. Water was dripping from Mrs. Riggs's dreary fedora, and it took her a while to focus on Mac and me. She appeared rather surprised to see we were wearing borrowed police-uniform jackets with badges on them.

Of course, we were wearing the uniforms over a motley assortment of our own dry clothes we'd retrieved from the zoo dormitory. Mac was sporting a police cap, too, but from what you could see of our hair we knew we didn't look better than a pair of drowned but determined rats.

"What happened?" Kim said. "Are you two all right?"

"We got a little wet," was all we said. The police jackets were too big on both Mac and me, and I could see Dr. Riggs was reading the front of my sweatshirt, another Aunt Doris had sent up with my sleeping bag. This one said IF THOU BE'ST NOT AN ASS, I AM A YOUTH OF FOURTEEN. Mac and I are really fifteen, but sometimes we make up different ages, depending on the circumstances.

Mrs. Riggs turned to Lieutenant Jamieson standing there in his mouse-gray double-breasted suit. "Did you get a break in the case?" she asked.

Jamieson stuttered, but then words began to flow despite his robotic control. "We need the kids a little longer," he said. "They say they can wind this up."

Kim and Dr. Riggs's heads swiveled back to us. "Oh," Kim said. "See, didn't I tell you they were smart?"

"Where do you want us?" Dr. Riggs said, looking exhausted and checking his watch.

"This way," Jamieson said, heading down the passageway and into the hospital annex. "If you both don't mind waiting there," he told Dr. and Mrs. Riggs, indicating the waiting area of the long white-tiled treatment room. The blood room sat like a dark cubicle at the other end of the room, and I could see Kim caught on fast that she and her husband were being excluded from the main event.

Jamieson shrugged. "We're juggling too many personalities as it is," he apologized. Perry stayed with Mac's parents. They would still be able to hear all the proceedings.

Mac, Jamieson, and I joined Zoode and a handful of armed cops who flanked Dr. Betty Waters, John Henning, and Peter Sandusky seated in the middle of the lab. There were some empty folding metal chairs opposite them, but Mac and I stood against the windowsill near the flooded geraniums. We had already given Perry and Lieutenant Jamieson an indication of the way things were going to shake down, but even Jamieson didn't know all the specifics. Mackenzie and I had been too busy doing the convoluted addition on the case, checking and rechecking right up to the last minute. Mac and I had gone over all the facts and clues we'd noted and seen. There was enough to point us in all the right directions and everything had fallen into place: we now knew why Ivan Allen was killed, exactly how, and by whom.

From the moment the police had driven us back from the jaguar area, we had less than an hour to pull together the hard evidence. We split up for some of that, and

Jesus had done his part and phoned in his results. He'd checked all the suspects out, and then some—overkilled as usual on social security numbers, business records, passport data, and pages of civil and criminal lawsuit info that had surrounded the Stuttgart tragedy. Mac held the folder with all our notes and data, including photos Jesus had e-mailed us; we had downloaded and printed them. They put faces on practically everyone who had been on the German zoo staff at the time of the fire.

Dr. Waters pointed her finger at us. "What are they doing here?" she demanded to know.

Lieutenant Jamieson sat down to face the trio. "They might be able to help us explain the death of Mr. Allen."

"That's absurd," Betty said.

"Yeah," Peter muttered.

"It's very clear what happened," Betty went on. "And it's very sad. A poor man mutilated by the fire in Germany deliberately set by Ivan Allen—that Stuttgart fire—poor, burned, disfigured Dr. Sandusky, lost his mind. Now you're making his grandson sit here—"

"I'm sorry—" Zoode said.

"Dr. Sandusky knew what Ivan was going to do," Betty said. "He was getting ready to set a fire to the Congo and collect the insurance money, just as he had fourteen years ago in Stuttgart. Dr. Sandusky had to stop him one way or the other."

Peter Sandusky started to tremble, and Betty put her

arm around him. It took a moment but he got it to-gether and was able to speak. "I only knew my grandpa after the fire. My parents had told me that the fire had twisted his mind. His pain, the burn scars. Years of skin grafts. The face my grandfather had to see in the mirror every morning . . ."

"We understand that," Lieutenant Jamieson said to the trio of suspects in a clear, no-nonsense voice. "Maimed, deranged doctor exacts revenge after four-teen years."

"And that's the truth," John Henning said quietly.

"Dr. Sandusky often watched Ivan from outside—watched him working late in the primate laboratory," Betty said, taking over as usual. "The doctor was obsessed with watching his every move. And it was the same last night. Toward dawn he saw Ivan take sugar by mistake and pass out—you know, go to sleep on one of the cots. Dr. Sandusky came into the lab and put Ivan's body in the outdoor jaguar habitat, knowing their gates would soon open for the morning. He counted on the jaguars' killing Ivan, but when they didn't, he found a way to take gorilla blood and somehow get it into the hospital.

"Don't forget, in his day before the fire, Dr. Sandusky was a primate researcher of the greatest magnitude. Sandusky knew how to draw blood from gorillas. He then must have slipped into the hospital and switched the blood. There's no mystery to it. It was so early. The rest of the staff had just woken up and come on duty. They were brewing coffee, thinking about doughnuts and—"

I interrupted Betty. "You want us to believe it was Dr. Sandusky alone who killed Ivan Allen."

"I'm not talking to you," Betty said coldly.

"Let the kids talk," said Lieutenant Jamieson. Mac and I smiled at him.

"From the get-go, I think everyone knew the murder of Ivan Allen was never the act of a single person," I continued calmly.

Henning loosened the collar on his work shirt.

"Even the killers helped reinforce the fact that there was, at the least, a pair of them," Mackenzie piped up.

"Yes," I said. "The racing pencil in the blood room—and coins all over the place. Of course, they didn't figure that Maxine Blessman would pick up the pencil, so that it almost wasn't even spotted."

Mac picked up from there. "The pencil pointed to Mohammed Jahangir—yes, Dr. Jahangir—and the coins in the jaguar and gorilla areas were supposed to mean that Franchot Lumet was not only busy jamming Coke and snack machines with his francs, but dropping them like mustard seeds all over the place while killing Ivan."

"It also meant the killers were amateurs," I said. "It didn't take us or Lieutenant Jamieson long, it turns out, to put together the sequence of events in Ivan's murder. Number one: Ivan was slipped sugar in his coffee.

Number two: The murderers waited for him to pass out, and then stuck him in the canopy crane bucket to lower his sleeping body into the jaguar area. That was why he had sap stains on his clothes."

Mac referred to her note pad. "Number three: The jaguars bit Ivan but didn't kill him," she said. "Number four: Someone took Ivan away from the jags and to the staff hospital, where it was obvious he'd need a transfusion. Number five: A hasty backup plan was improvised—one of the killers sedated Gargantua and collected a pint of his blood. Number six: The blood is brought to the hospital. Number seven: Ivan Allen received the gorilla blood instead of human blood—and dies surely and quickly from the wrong agglutinogens."

"We're saying a *team* killed Ivan Allen," Mackenzie said.

"Your team," I told Betty.

"What a bizarre theory," Betty said. She stared at me and Mac with more hate in her eyes than anyone we'd ever seen.

"That includes you, John Henning, Peter, and his grandfather," I insisted. "The four of you each did your own little part in murdering Ivan."

Betty laughed. She looked to the others—even to Perry, and Mac's parents who were watching from the waiting area and listening to everything. Ms. Waters seemed to expect at least someone would laugh with her at the absurdity. But no one did. "At least you acknowledge that poor Dr. Sandusky was one of the killers," she said, with a peculiar logic. "You'll learn soon enough he was the only one."

"She's right," Peter said. "He was my grandfather, but he acted alone."

"No, Peter," I said. "*You* are one of the killers. Your grandfather was guilty only of infecting all of you with a hatred of Ivan Allen that made all his killers lose a sense of reality. The murderers are all people or relatives of people who were hurt at Stuttgart or heard the animals being burned alive. Dr. Sandusky made certain all of you would 'Remember Paterfamilias'—meaning not one of you nor Ivan Allen should forget the horrible thing he did. He wrote the notes through the years, so fittingly etched in charcoal. Your grandfather was guilty only of being a longtime cheerleader to the team. A cheerleader for murder."

## 14

### Even If You Win the Rat Race, You're Still a Rat

**Betty's face looked like she was thinking** twice before speaking so she could say something twice as nasty. She inched her chair forward as though the repositioning would give her more power. "Thank God, our American courts don't act on zany trial balloons like the one you're sending up," she said to us. "In the United States there is a requirement of hard evidence."

"Oh, there's enough of that," I said. "First of all— well, let's start with Peter. Peter had a problem after he had replaced the pint of stored Ivan blood with the gorilla blood. He had to get rid of the empty pouch, or at least hide it until he could get rid of it later."

"You're off base," Peter said, his voice cracking.

"The police hadn't found it, and I don't think we would have found it either," Mackenzie said, "if I didn't like plants." She reached out and stroked the leaves of the nearest geranium plant. "I had noticed right off the bat this morning how all the plants were draining nicely in their pots on the windowsills, except for the poor geraniums. Something was interfering with their draining."

Mac eased the plant and its perfect cylinder of a root mass up from the pot. She slipped out a folded translucent, plastic bag from the bottom of the pot.

"Something like the empty blood bag," I said.

"Not this bag," Mac said. "This is just a stand-in."

"We had Lieutenant Jamieson retrieve the actual blood bag from the pot," I said. "The bag that had a few drops of gorilla blood left in it and your fingerprints all over it, Peter. You were careless enough to handle the ape-blood switcheroo without wearing gloves."

We didn't wait for Peter to admit or deny anything, knowing he was nailed. Henning was another story.

"You drove the crane," Mac said to the groundskeeper. "Somehow, you—probably with the help and direction of someone else on the team—got Ivan's narcoleptic body into the bucket and placed it in the jaguar area."

"You're the only one who really knows how to drive that thing," I said. "You have the key. It takes a lot of practice to control the telescoping hydraulics of the bucket arm."

"You can't prove it was me," Henning said.

"Actually, you're right, we can't," I said. "But we did give it a lot of thought. You see, Mr. Henning, there's one thing a lot of people do. They underestimate smart and dynamic celebrities. They think they're just egoists and balloons of hot, lucky air. But that's not been our experience. Mac and I have noticed that acclaimed, truly accomplished people usually achieve what they do because they're made of tough stuff."

"You can hate them," Mac said. "And they can be vicious and evil and rotten. . . ."

"And Ivan Allen was all of that, we're sure," I said. "But he was smarter than you, Mr. Henning. I tried to put myself in his place. I've had sugar. I can feel the sleep coming on—and so I lie down. I, Ivan Allen, go to sleep—and when I wake up I'm on the ground . . . and there is a jaguar who has me by the throat. . . ."

"What are you saying?" Henning asked.

"You're sounding crazy," Betty snarled.

"What I'm trying to tell you, Mr. Henning," I said, "is that you are missing a button from your shirt—the missing button Mac and I noticed the first time you descended in your bucket. Well, Mac and I wondered what happened to it, and we knew it could have very well come off when you were lugging Ivan Allen's body in and out of the bucket. It could have fallen on the ground, which as it turns out it *did*."

Sergeant Zoode spoke up. "P.C. and Mac had us look for it."

"Even with his throat in a jaguar's mouth," Mac said, "Ivan Allen was smart and determined enough to some-how get the button from your shirt into his own pocket—which is where it was found. Swift and celebrated people don't die easily. Oh, you won't be getting the electric chair because of any old button."

Henning shuddered because, I guessed, he knew what more had to be said. "Your daughter was Wilma," I said. "Wilma Henning. She was in charge of the breeding program in Stuttgart. You all knew that might come out easily if the police got into the whole Stuttgart history. Wilma was listed in so many of the articles. She was brave. . . ."

Mr. Henning began to weep. "She was very—yes, brave—"

I went on. "The articles mention how she went in to the burning nursery, how she tried to save the babies, the young chimps. There were a couple of newborn lowland gorillas. . . ."

I shut up.

We all—even Betty—let John Henning weep. He fought to pull himself back together. Finally, he found words. "Wilma couldn't save them. She heard their cries. Oh, God, my daughter lost her mind. Ivan Allen made her lose her mind."

Mac and I both turned to Betty. "You said you were never in Germany," I said.

"She told us that, too," Sergeant Zoode said, checking his clipboard notes.

"I wasn't there," Betty repeated.

"Well, *Betty Waters* wasn't there," I said. "But Mac and I went over the list of the staff very carefully. The week before the fire an American intern had arrived. She was assigned to Wilma, to help in the nursery, as part of a study-abroad program for her junior year at Wesleyan University."

"The intern's name was Elise Wasser," Mac said.

"I didn't pick it up when I first saw the list of the German staff," I said. "But when we went over the list more carefully, I realized that Elise is another form of the name 'Elizabeth'—and another form of the name 'Betty.' And, of course, *Wasser* is German for 'water.'"

Mac opened our folder with Jesus' data and downloads and showed a picture of the young intern who was in Stuttgart for the one week before the fire. She passed the photo for everyone to see.

"'Elise Wasser' means *Betty Waters*," I said.

Betty began to shake. "I wasn't going to forget," she said quietly. "Never. I vowed never to forget."

There was silence for a few moments, before Lieutenant Jamieson gave the signal. Policemen moved to closely flank Peter, Henning, and Betty as they stood. They started out in silence, but suddenly Betty spun around and screamed at Mac and me.

"And what did you think?" Betty said, anger nearly choking her. "We should have followed up through the courts? We should have appealed to the police for justice? Gone to newspapers and magazines? You think there was another way to do it, another way to fix Ivan Allen for what he did? Don't you know how ludicrous all of you are! How weak the laws are? Our whole legal system is pathetic and corrupt and useless. We'd be better off without it."

"No," Mac said.

"She's right," I seconded my pal. "Without any law you know what this world would be? A jungle."

For a moment Betty looked like an animal ready to break loose and attack us. She glanced toward the waiting room and locked eyes with Mrs. Riggs. Kim was on her feet, her fedora cocked, ready to charge like an enraged lioness to protect her cubs.

It had stopped raining by the time the Riggs clan and I had been escorted out of the building by Lieutenant Jamieson and Sergeant Zoode. There was a lot of thank-you's and chit-chat, so it was past midnight before Mac and I were nestled in the back of the Riggses' station wagon and her parents were driving out of the Fordham gates and away from the zoo. It was Dr. and Mrs. Riggs who were wide awake now, while Mackenzie and I quickly covered ourselves with our opened sleeping bags. We must have looked like a couple of crashing Eskimos in quilts, but we didn't care.

Kim was driving and kept an eye on us in the rearview mirror. "You guys did a great job," she said. And she had only heard the half of it. We figured all the grisly details like Gargantua playing war-ball with us could be left for the next day.

"We're glad it worked out," I said.

"That's a positive," Mackenzie muttered.

The Riggses certainly caught on fast that Mac and I wanted to snooze, so they just had a nice fiery chat between themselves about dry cleaning, which escalated to major proportions by the time we reached the entrance to the George Washington Bridge and turned south onto the West Side Highway.

Mackenzie let out a sigh that quieted her parents. Kim glanced into the rearview mirror with concern. "Are you two all right back there?' she asked.

"Yeah," Mackenzie mumbled. "I was just thinking about the lesson I learned at the zoo today . . ."

"What, honey?" Kim asked.

"Oh," Mac said, giving me a little punch in the arm. "I guess it's just that . . . at least the way I see it now is . . . when you're in a jungle, it doesn't matter who shops for the pickle."